CUTOFF

MICHAEL LEE

Cover concept: Michael Lee
Cover and interior design: – Sharon Kizziah-Holmes

Chief Editor: Kate Richards,
Content and line editor: Laura Garland. Nanette Sipe.

Publishing Coordinator – Sharon Kizziah-Holmes

Paperback-Press
an imprint of A & S Publishing
Paperback Press, LLC
Springfield, Missouri

ISBN -13: 978-1-964559-91-9

DEDICATION

I have to say a word about my friend, David Angelle. Many years ago, he said, "Doc, you need to put me in one of your books." He grinned that rapacious smile of his. I couldn't say no.

Da'vid Angelle in "Cutoff" bears no resemblance in character to the real David Angelle, who is big man that worked on the Mississippi River as an engineer on tugboats and has seen some rough times. I used his size and manner of speaking to make a villain worthy of him. No one has a kinder heart.

Thanks for the suggestion, my friend. I know you will love being a villain. I still hear the coon ass in your voice."Kiii yaaa." I hope you love the book.

WHAT PEOPLE ARE SAYING ABOUT MICHEAL'S BOOKS

"Lee writes a multi-level story, drawing you into the characters, wondering what happens next."
5 stars

"Loved Michael Lee's, 'McKinzey's Revenge'. A great western story involving all the elements of a real page turner, from horse thieves, to shoot-em-ups to an Indian vision quest, to references to the character's Irish roots. Well done." 5 stars

"A morality tale about revenge," 5 stars

"This book is subtle as it drew me in, and I like where that it took place somewhere other than the dusty areas of the southwest. It contained all of the things a person loves about a good western." 4 stars

"I'll kill them, Pa. I'll kill them all." and kill them he did. Savagely, brutally, and without mercy. In a page turning rampage, he almost loses his own soul in the carnage, but is saved by the magic realism of a friendly Native American shaman. Michael Lee writes a western worth the ride." 5 stars

"This is one of the finest westerns I have ever read! Set in the North West. I learned about the Shoshone, and mining camps, I had never read. Clearly well researched, with powerful phrases. It is a novel of revenge, love, and family loyalty! 5 stars

Acknowledgments

I always have to give a shout out to my writing support: My Critique Me Friday 6 i.e. Straw Boss Skiz (Sharon Kizziah-Holmes), Thriller Beast (John Cawlfield), Reigning Regency Queen (Conetta Taylor), Mystery Romancer (Shirley King McCann), Lori Copeland (Romance Icon). My Best Always...Pick-A-Toe Joe

Special mention...Clarissa Willis

Of course my friends and family and last but not least, my readers. Thank you for your support and kind words of encouragement. They keep me writing.

Introduction

The Sublette (Greenwood) Cutoff was a short cut for pilgrims in the 1850's. Most followed the Green River south to Jim Bridger's Fort to rest and re-supply. That would add an extra two to three weeks on the Oregon Trail.

By taking the Cutoff, travelers saved a lot of time, especially if they were late in the season. No one wanted to be caught out on the trail during blizzards and cold weather when game and water were scarce.

However the Sublette Cutoff was sixty mean miles over sagebrush desert. No water, no grass, no actual trail. They simply headed west. They had to carry water and fodder for their animals.

The Mormon push carters had it tougher as they had much less room to carry essentials, let alone extra water and food. Many did not make it or were simply lost in a vast wilderness of nothing if they lost their bearings. Sadly, the human condition has a vacancy filled by human predators. Lawless men were rampant. As civilization moved in, lawlessness moved out. That is what this story is about.

CHAPTER 1

Oregon City was two days' ride on the Barlow Road as it snaked out of the mountains and descended the lower western slopes of Mount Hood. Shepherd's mind reached back to the last assignment he had just finished. He was hot and dusty. Strong sunlight shone down in midafternoon intensity as he and his horse, Dusty, rode out of the forest, feeling drowsy and complacent. It would not do to give Lyle Newton anything less than a complete report of the apprehension of the highwaymen he had just put in jail at the fort in Dulles on the Columbia River. He dozed in the saddle.

"All right, me bucko, that's far enough. Me and Granny got you covered."

A Scottish-tinged voice broke his reverie of thought, resounding from the rocks on his left.

His mind snapped back in a jolt, he jerked his head up, jammed his feet into his stirrups, stopped his horse, and raised his hands. Turning his head slightly to his left, he peeked from beneath the brim of his hat. The voice had come from the rocks along the trail.

A smile broke across his face. "I'm friendly. I can smell your fire. It's a ways off, but I smell your coffee. It would be good to have some conversation. I've been on the trail for a while." Shepherd kicked his feet free of his stirrups and stretched his legs and arms, letting go a deep yawn. He wanted to seem at ease but deep down, he felt foolish for being surprised like this.

"You don't look like a Hudson man. Why you a following along for me?"

A shotgun nudged Shepherd's right knee causing him to jump at the touch. "How'd you do that?" Shepherd looked back to his right. "I swore you were in the rocks on the other side, above me."

"I've stayed alive by being in places I wasn't supposed to be, Blacky. Let me have a look at ye. What you doing out here by yourself? They a white man coming after you I bet. You're going ta bring me trouble?"

"I'm on my own. Nobody looking for me." Shepherd leaned over and looked his assailant in the face. "Nobody owns me, Mister. Put that gun away. I'm not after you. Who the hell are you anyway?" Shepherd was looking at a stout florid man with ruddy-red hair, a full beard, and sharp piercing eyes. He was dressed in rough boots and a full-length green wool greatcoat. A ten-gauge shotgun held in his gnarled fists pointed unwaveringly at Shepherd's middle.

"What are ya, Blacky? There ain't many free nigras riding around this territory. I thought there was only runaways over ta this side."

"Name's Shepherd. I'm a United States Deputy Marshal, headed back to Salem for my next assignment."

"A deputy marshal to boot? You are full of surprises. A man hunter, ya say?"

"If need be. I go where Lyle Newton and the Territory of Oregon tells me to go and what to do, whether it concerns man or beast. That's the job."

"So, you got no association with da Hudson men in any shape or form?"

"Other than running into them on the trail and their

supply trains, either delivering goods or hauling back plume. Seem like fine fellas. Never give me no trouble." Shepherd cut off a small chew, offered some to the man on the trail, who turned it down with a shake of his head.

"Well, all right, then. Get down! Wait! You got a badge or some bona fide's?" The Scot motioned with his shotgun. "Be careful now, Granny is sensitive."

Shepherd sat up, unbuttoned his jacket, then flipped open the lapel of his coat and pulled out his warrants. "I bought the badge in Dulles. A jeweler made it for me. Got my name on it." A bright brass marshal's star was pinned to his coat.

"Lean over here's so's I can see it. I'm not as sharp-eyed as I used to be."

Shepherd leaned over so the gunman could see more clearly. As he did so, he grabbed the heavy collar of the man's coat and pulled it up over his face. The barrel of the gun came up when the coat did, and Shepherd jerked it out of the assailant's hand and pushed him into the side of the trail with his foot.

Tripping over a large rock, the man yelped, lost his balance, and fell headfirst into the brush, onto his nose with toes pointed down atop the rocks that had tripped him.

"Now that's a fine thing," the rugged man swore. "Well, bloody Christ! Help me up, will you now? It's no a pretty picture with my arse up in the air and me nose in the ground." As much as he tried, the red-bearded man could not get his feet under him.

Shepherd climbed down from Dusty and again grabbed the collar of the man's coat and drug him up onto the trail where he struggled to his feet.

"You're an uncommon one, Blackie. A white man might a shot me, whilst he had de chance."

"I am uncommon. Don't call me Blackie. Name is Shepherd. I don't have the uncommon pleasure of knowing your name. Truce?"

"Hmmm. Aye, truce." The redheaded man stepped forward. "Phineas Sinclair is my name. Don't call me Phin." He offered his hand.

Shepherd shook hands with him. Phineas jerked Granny back out of Shepherd's relaxed grip and pointed it back at him.

"See 'ere Blackie, you should not be so trusting of a stranger."

Shepherd stood still. "I thought we called a truce? You going back on your word?"

Phineas studied him for a full minute. "You're right. I gave me word." He lowered his gun. "I got coffee and a haunch a mutton a broiling on da spit. It might be spoilt and burnt by now, but you're welcome to what I got. You're an uncommon man, as I said. I think I like you. I owe you."

"You could have shot me as well. Let's call it even, shall we? Oh, you might need these if another situation arises and you feel threatened." Shepherd tossed him the caps he had taken off of the shotgun's nipples. He knew it wouldn't shoot without them.

"What! I say, Blackie, I do like you. You're a careful man, like me. I might take you into me heart and love ya like a brother." Phineas replaced the caps, looked at Shepherd, and chuckled to himself.

Phineas led the way off of the trail along a path that was so faint Shepherd barely recognized it as having been traveled by anyone. The camp was well secreted. The smell of smoke and roasting leg of mutton intensified within steps of the camp.

Phineas was a canny man, Shepherd could see this immediately as he studied the layout of the camp. His horse and pack animal were picketed down a bank close to grass and water. Panniers close by were ready for instant escape. A water shedding lean-to, constructed from brush and fallen branches, was built so the heat of the fire would keep him warm. A supply of wood lay piled within easy reach.

Fir boughs covered by a bearskin served as his sleeping bed. All in all, a tidy neat camp, well-hidden off of the main trail. Shepherd guessed Phineas could hole up in this spot indefinitely.

"Sit down, Shepherd. Make yourself ta home. There's coffee, you can help yourself to mutton. I got some biscuits in the pan covered with leaves and beans are simmering by da fire."

Shepherd used his bowie knife to slice off some of the mutton. It smelled good. He sprinkled some salt over the sizzling meat from a nearby dish and spooned beans onto his plate. His curiosity got the better of him and he peeked under the big leaves covering the pan of biscuits. His eyes widened in surprise. Beautiful, golden, plump biscuits sat there. A yellow lump of butter was wrapped in a large maple tree leaf. Shepherd cut off a large knob of butter and spread it on two plump golden puffs of biscuit. He was impressed.

"You live well, Phineas. Thanks for the grub. I get tired of my own cooking while on the trail. Fresh butter is a treat. You got a cow hidden somewhere?"

"You never mind where things come from. You just enjoy my hospitality, if you don't mind. I don't show me camp to many people, if you know what I mean, let alone telling you ma name."

In between mouthfuls, the two men appraised each other without talking. They were pretty much equals in age as well as skills in staying alive. Instinctively, they appreciated the other.

In a man's life, there are rare times when men accept each other. They ask no questions of their past or question their intentions in the now. It is a sterling moment that passes between men, that acceptance. It happened to Shepherd and

Phineas, an unspoken bond set in between them, deeper than kinship, mysterious and unspoken in its formation and complexity. Whatever the future may bring, these men would be friends. No matter what side they were on, no matter the circumstances, their friendship would stand.

Shepherd was the first to speak. "So who you hiding from? He wiped out his plate, washed it in a pan of hot water warming by the fire. Then he placed it among the forks of a large branch stuck in the dirt to hold Phineas' pots and pans, keeping them off of the ground

"It's a long story."

"I've got all night. I'm not due back in Salem for a few days. I have a full stomach. Compliments to the chef. The biscuits were marvels of perfection, by the way."

"Scots invented the biscuit. Though, I should a' tell you that those little cakes you just had, were more like a sweet cake than a biscuit. Real biscuit is hard as hell's laughter and tough to chew. A proper biscuit could break your teeth. Biscuits in America is more like a poorly made scone, ta me."

"However, you may call it. It was delicious. So…who are you hiding from? The Hudson men? The British? You're not a wanted man in my jurisdiction or I would know about you. I hope I never see your name on any of our lists of wanted men."

"I'm a Scot."

"I can tell."

"My family goes back in history for many generations clear to the time afore it was ever written down. Our Clan has fought the English, the Welsh, the Irish, the great fierce Norsemen from icy Denmark, and more recently the whole of the damn British Empire; always holding our own, mind ye. The British Empire is financed through the Hudson Bay

Trading Company in this part of the world, trading in furs and wood from these forests. East India Tea Company finances the rest of the empire on the other side of the world."

"I know of the reputation of the Hudson Bay Company. The United States may go to war with them over the Oregon Territory." Shepherd's interest perked up. It would be interesting to see if any of Phineas' story would affect his territory. Information was a valued commodity.

"Righto, me bucko. Anyways, my problem started when I had traveled down into the bosom of the English capital in London on some business matter. Have I told ye how much we hate the English? I was having a dram or two with my English friends, and the next moment I remember, I woke aboard a Hudson Bay ship bound for Canada. The bloody whoremongers shanghaied me. My trusted English friends had sold me off to the Hudson Bay men.

"I loathe the bloody English!"

"Ended up at Vancouver, unloading freight, from the very ship they imprisoned me on. It was work or have me throat cut and thrown to the fish. When I got ma chance, I smashed the back of the bloody captain's head in with an axe handle and fought my way out of the fort into the wilderness with nothing but the clothes on me back. Lived with the Indians for a year and then I started my revenge."

"Revenge? What could you do?" Shepherd smiled to himself at the thought of one man waging war on the British.

"I learnt their trading routes and the times they ran their mule trains and where warehouses were hidden. Then I robbed 'em. Stole everything I could lay me hands on."

"Do you have a warehouse? A place to hide all those goods? It's not around here... No, don't tell me, I don't want to know."

"Have a dram of whisky my friend?" Phineas studied Shepherd with a long look before he dug a bottle of whisky out from the fir boughs under his bear skin. He set the bottle down then dug deeper, pulling out a well-appointed wooden box. With reverence which lit up his face, he revealed four crystal glasses cuddled in red velvet nestled inside. A soft cotton cloth was folded to the side. With a flourish, he flipped the cloth open and polished two of the precious crystal glasses. Holding one up to the sun, looking for imperfections, the sun rays glinted off the cut crystal surface in bright rainbow hues. He looked at Shepherd for an appreciation of this revered moment.

"Finest kiss of the angels, this is. Bes water dis side of heaven. Speyside. Stuff they make here is piss. Scot's invented whisky an' give it to the world. This beautiful bottle of sweet angel sweat is made at a wee distillery just this side of where I used to live. Stored and aged back ta home in the bog of the moors. The damn English bring it here and I steal it from them. It's my favorite. I have a glass for ye. Got to have a crystal glass. Do you know how to take it? Do you know the proper way to drink a man's whisky?"

"I thought I did," replied Shepherd, no longer sure if he did or not.

A look of pure delight bloomed across Phineas' face as he spoke, "Just a wee drop of crystal pure water into your whiskey, helps open the fleavers. Here, try a sip without the water."

Shepherd sipped, not sure what he was doing or supposed to be tasting. He simply knew that this was not the time to annoy the Scot. "Hmm. It's good." His eyes followed every step of this initiation.

"Now with water." Phineas tippled a few drams of clear water into his glass.

The student sipped again. Appreciation spread across his face. "It is better. It's as if a flower has opened from a bud. It's wonderful. It has a perfume."

"See, much better, isn't it?" With great care, as if

performing a holy rite, the Scot refilled the crystal glass, added the proper amount of water, and handed Shepherd a full glass. "Here's to your health, Blackie."

Shepherd started to protest but thought better of it. There was no rancor in the man's words. The whisky worked its magic as a mild warmth flowed through his body. He didn't mind what this Scot called him. The words didn't feel offensive, coming from his newfound friend.

"I sell ma treasures off to da highest buyer or I give to poor people who are in need. Usually, I sell to the American fur traders, sometimes to Indians. They all need the same supplies as the English. Did I tell you how much I hate the booggerin' English? Have another?"

It was excellent whisky and better with a drop or two of water. Shepherd had never had such fine drink. He accepted Phineas' offer with glad heart. He did not ask where it came from and did not want to know. The fire was warm. He felt content. Phineas' company was bright and witty. Shepherd listened to him talk on into the night. He was quite an unusual man, this Phineas Sinclair.

CHAPTER 2

———◆—◇◆◇—◆———

Shepherd was waiting in the office for Lyle when he returned after his morning coffee at Becky's. "Morning, Lyle, just got in. Becky's busy? I'm going for breakfast just as soon as I make my report. Those highwaymen on the Barlow Road are taken care of. I had to shoot two of them, wounded one, killed one, one gave up and shot the other one when the shotgun he threw down discharged. He was all bloodied, heading into Indian country when I last saw him. The two we captured are cooling their heels in a cell at the fort.

Captain Shelton there in charge was glad to have that cleared up. The army had been chasing them for months. They're languishing in a cold cell, with only mush and coffee to eat. He'll hold them for trial in a few weeks."

"Sounds like another good job, Shepherd. Go get some breakfast and file your report back to me when you're finished. I've got another assignment for you."

"Anything close by? My butt is sore from being days in the saddle. Hair won't grow back there anymore."

Lyle smiled. "I know what ya mean. I've spent my time in the saddle too. No, I'm afraid I've got you headed back into desert country over by the South Pass and the Green River territory. Same story though, bandits raiding

10

settlers trying to make it through the Greenwood Cutoff. Reports of robbery, murder, rape, and kidnapping. An organized gang is working the area. We need to bring them in. I'll have your writs and warrants ready when you come back."

"Now, that's depressing. Better let me go, while I can still have an appetite for Becky's good food. See you in a little while."

"Hey, I bought this badge. A nice brass one. Jeweler made it for me. Got my name on it." He opened his lapel to show Lyle.

Lyle smiled in return. "Territory don't issue badges yet. People is always wanting to see a badge. I guess it helps show who you are. I need to get one myself."

Shepherd walked down the sidewalk toward Becky's café. Salem was growing. The new capital was a bustin' its britches from all the pilgrims and businesses coming in, glad to be at the end of their trail. This was everyone's first stop after they made it by land or sea over the northern routes. From the south, most immigrants were coming up the Applegate Trail, either for the gold fields in California or the rich lands of the Willamette Valley.

He pushed open the doors to Becky's Café and was immediately greeted.

"Morning, Shepherd. Good to see you back. How'd it go? Did you get your man?" Becky upturned a coffee cup and poured a welcome cup from the granite blue pot she held and pushed it in front of him.

"Morning, Becky. Good to see you. It is good to get back. Yep. I always get my man or men. Don't seem to be an end to bad men, no matter what part of the country you go to. What's been happening here? I know you catch all the local news."

Becky placed a white cake decorated with blue icing in her display case. She stopped for a minute to think what she should say. "Got gold strikes up and down the coast.

Indians are mad because the miners think they have the right to whatever they want. The miners really feel a dead Indian is a good Indian. They've killed men, women, and children from many of the coastal tribes, searching for gold wherever they want. The whole countryside is like a dry forest just waiting for lightning to strike."

"So, more bad men to go after. Seems like nothin' is better, it just gets worse." Shep walked over to a table and sat down. Becky followed with a pot of coffee. She flipped over a blue and white china cup sitting upside down on a saucer and filled it.

"Well, you're good at your job. Be careful out there. Ready to order?"

"You bet. I'll have my usual, okay?"

"Comin' right away. Six eggs, sunny-side up. A side of bacon and one of ham with a short stack of pancakes and four biscuits with jam and butter, sliced tomatoes, and onions. Heard anything from Jonny? I bet he's married that Shoshone girl he was so in love with, by now. I wish I could have been there. He had better bring that bride in for me to look over. I consider myself one of the family, you know. Anything else?"

"I wish we both could have been there. Just wasn't in the cards for us, Becky. I can guarantee you. You'll like Laughing Grass. She will need a friend when Jon brings her home. She has only lived with her tribe. I look for Jon to come home sometime in the spring, bringing her to the ranch. She will feel a little lost for a while. Thanks for the coffee. No, nothing else, just bring it on. I've been looking forward to one of your meals, been on the trail too long. Lyle's going to send me out again, from what he says. I need to go out to the ranch and check on the stock. The house should be completely finished by now."

"I've been having Burt ride out every so often to check on things. Looks like everything is fine. I went out last Sunday to see the house. It is beautiful, room enough for all of you, but I know you'll want to go check yourself. Drink your coffee. Clem will have your breakfast in a few minutes."

◆◦◆◦◆

Shepherd took his time riding out to the ranch, many memories welled up in his mind as he passed Kalapua rock, a local landmark. His stepfather, John McKinzey, had been killed out here, a little over a year ago. A devastating loss for himself and Jonny, John McKinzey's son. He was known to his friends as Mack. But there were also wonderful memories as well. Together, they had carved this place out of the wilderness after their long initiation into the West on the Oregon Trail. They had built a home for themselves, a grist mill to grind the grain for bread, and stock feed raised by the newcomers. They had set up corrals, pounded the posts into the ground with their bare hands and the sweat of their bodies for the horses, and they ran cattle in the forests as the land was cleared. The MCK brand was an established brand in the valley.

Mack McKinzey had been killed in a night raid by the Nolans, their mortal enemy. They had not rebuilt the sawmill after it had burned down that night. Jon had settled the blood feud by killing everyone in Nolan's gang. Now, those hard days were past. Jon had gone back to the Shoshone nation to marry Laughing Grass. They were expected back in the spring. Shepherd had gone from being orphaned then adopted by the McKinzeys, to being appointed a United States Deputy Marshal. He and Jon shared ownership of the ranch and mill as equal partners. Life had a mysterious way of unraveling itself.

He stopped on a rise as he surveyed the ranch. It never stopped enthralling him. The smell of the looming winter touched Shepherd's nose. The green forests seemed like home and the weariness he felt in his bones after his last

13

job seemed to melt away, the closer he got. He looked forward to seeing their new home, which was being built when Jonny left for his bride. They should be finished by now. The grist mill was back in operation, run by Marcus, who had taken over the miller's job like a duck takes to water. It felt good to come home.

He looked forward to a fire on this chilly night, sitting in front of his own hearth, a good meal in his belly, but first, he had to see how everything was progressing. As he sat on Dusty, watching the waterwheel turn, he could hear the timbers groaning as the great stones ground the grain. The Willamette River flowed to the north, emptying into the wild Columbia River gorge before it spilt into the sea. Their ranch sat in the background behind the mill, corrals to the side of the house, barn in the back. The entrance, a timber-covered cupola with a large porch and two huge front doors inviting one to enter. Still green fields were dotted with fat red cattle and the horses they had raised. Clouds scudded across the deep blue sky. He had come home. He looked forward to Jon coming back home, bringing his bride. He missed him. Wistfully, he appreciated that something else was missing. His heart yearned for something he had never had. A wife. Maybe that part of him would be filled one of these days. All things seemed to come in time if you put the effort into it.

The land felt to be at peace. This was his home. Their home. He rode down the hill, up the lane, and opened the door. Becky hadn't told him she had brought in furniture. There were armchairs, a divan, a table, and chairs. Nice pieces to have, until the newlyweds could pick out what they wanted. It felt like a home. He'd add some touches to his part of the house.

Becky had a bed and a chest of drawers for him in his bedroom. Shepherd built a fire in the hearth in the main living room and looked about him admiring his longtime friend's taste in furniture. He slipped his boots off onto a red oriental carpet, before sprawling back on the butter-soft leather divan. Before he knew it, he had fallen asleep, warmed by the fire of his new hearth.

"The house is finished. Marcus is working the mill full-time. Old Tom is coming by and helping out. Cattle are getting fat. Sections of their property are being logged. Everything is in order." Shepherd said out loud his list of things he wanted to see get done as he rode back to town. He was satisfied about his home and now was ready to leave any time to do Lyle's errand at the Sublette cutoff. Damn, he didn't want to do it. Too much riding again, so soon after another long trip, but that was the job.

Joseph, the family attorney, was waiting for him when he opened the door to Lyle's office.

"Hell-o, Joe. What brings you around here?"

"Good news, Shepherd. Remember the Exclusion bill I told you about? That will only apply to Negros just entering the territory. If you are here already, there is no exclusion."

"I still think it's damn unfair. We are seeking freedom and free land, just like any white citizen. What the hell is wrong with everybody? What are they afraid of?"

"People are afraid of the unknown, Shep. Believe me, I feel the same way you do. I come from a land where your nationality is always challenged. I had to leave because of it. In time, it will change."

"What about that Lash law? Will it be changed?"

"There's already a movement started to repeal that law. No one liked it to begin with. They felt to use it as an incentive to the Exclusion bill. The Lash law will never be enforced, is the word I am getting from my friends in the legislature."

"Should not have been written in the first place. Have you ever seen anyone lashed, whipped? It's not a pretty sight, Joe."

"Yes, I have, Shepherd. In the old country, the lash was used often, as it was on the high seas. I watched a man being punished on the ship I came across on, just because he did not salute a superior officer. It's not just a problem for this country, but a worldwide problem."

The sheriff cleared his throat to interrupt. "Ahem, gentlemen, I appreciate your concerns, but I have to run this office. I'm glad that law doesn't pertain to you, Shepherd. This community thinks well of you. I think well of you and right now I want your sorry hide figuring out what to do when you get to the Greenwood Cutoff. They are also calling it the Sublette Cutoff for the men who rode it the first time. Any ideas?" Lyle tossed some papers to Shepherd.

"Those are the reports on what's happened so far. Settlers are heading into the desert traveling on the cutoff and not coming out on the other side. Wagons are found burnt, bodies riddled with arrows or shot. People are missing without explanation. It may be Indians or someone wanting us to think its Indians. We need to do something. Read those. Make a plan. I will be back in an hour and I want to know what you want to do and a time frame for doing it. If I don't hear back from you within that time frame, I'll need to send someone after you. I don't want to send someone after you. I want you back with this gang or the Indians responsible in jail or dead." Lyle closed the door behind him.

Shepherd looked at Joe after perusing the reports. "Know anything about this Greenwood, or Sublette Cutoff? I've only been by there once, while we were headed to Bridger's fort."

"I can't help you there, Shepherd. I came over by ship."

"I'll go ask around. Maybe some of the new emigrants will know someone or something that can help. By the way,

I met a fella, said his name was Stuart same as you."

"I have an uncle. You met Phineas? Not many people have even seen Phineas."

"Drank some scotch with him. Spent the night in his camp. A mighty interesting man, your uncle."

"Glory be. I'm stunned." Joseph looked at Shepherd with an inquisitive eye.

"Did he tell you how he came to be here?"

"Yes, he did. Got shanghaied in London. I suppose that is one of the reasons you're here as well. Something to do with his kidnapping."

"That's right. I started making inquiries after he disappeared. I soon learned that if I didn't keep my mouth shut, I'd end up dead or wake up on some boat bound for the South China Sea. I came here looking for him."

"He's quite the man. I'm glad I don't have to take after him. If you see him, remind him to keep his business with the Hudson Bay Company on their side of the border, will you? I'm headed over to the smithies. Dusty has a loose shoe. Maybe the smith has heard some news about the cutoff from some new pilgrims. See you later."

Shepherd spent the rest of the morning talking to Milo Brennan, the local blacksmith. He made inquiries at local merchants and talked to bartender friends that he had in the local saloons. Most of the reports reflected what other travelers had seen or heard. There was a problem and he had to be the fixer. He made arrangements for supplies. He had ground flour and maize from his own mill as well as a good supply of jerky. He rounded out his foodstuffs with desiccated vegetables, dry soup, coffee, beans, dry fruit, bacon, and a dry cured ham, sugar, and canned milk. He was ready to go as soon as he made his plans known to Lyle.

"I read over those reports, Lyle, and made some inquiries of my own. I made up a temporary plan of action. It's there on your desk. I expect to be gone about six to eight weeks. Deposit my pay for me when it comes in, will you? I'm packed up and ready to go."

"Be careful, Shepherd. I got word Randy Smith got killed over by the California border in some damn gold camp. Indians have been seeking revenge when their people are killed. Trouble is, it's usually is not the ones who did the killing, who get killed in return. All white men look alike, I guess. Besides the killings, the Indians are upset, 'cause the gold camps are ruining the water and killing the fish and game. Don't blame them much. I have to break the news to Cindy, just the same. Don't know who done it. Hardest part of the job. Headed over there now."

"Randy was a good man. This is a hard life to understand sometimes, Lyle. Too many senseless killings on both sides. He was one of the best. I looked up to him. My sympathies lie with the Indians. No one respects that it is their land; has been for thousands of years. Most of the new people see something and just take it with no regard, that the natives have been here for generations. I hope it doesn't get worse. The governor needs to step in and put a stop to it. Trouble is, he's just as greedy as the prospectors. See you in eight weeks. I'll stop in to see Cindy on my way out of town."

Shepherd planned to go to the Greenwood Cutoff backward. The crossing at Names Hill was where everyone was crossing the Green River after coming out of the desert. From what he had learned, the gang hung out at a place called Angelles. This was a local bar, café, and general store set up to supply emigrants before they started the arduous desert trek near the parting of ways. Angelles was the last water for fifty miles. Everyone stopped there.

He avoided company when he was on the hunt. Solitude made his mind sharper and his senses more acute. He didn't want anyone surprising him, like Phineas had done. Lesson learned. There would be the typical questions he would ask at local gathering places and saloons of course, hoping to glean any new tidbits, but he didn't linger anywhere.

Sooner or later, his skin color would come up and Shepherd would try to talk sense into the head of some sneering galloot, trying to make a reputation off of a cowering black man. More often than not, he would have to lay the barrel of his gun across someone's head to convince them he would only take so much crap from them. He flashed his badge after all efforts for a peaceful end to intimidation failed. As time went on, his name became more familiar and was sometimes enough to dissuade the local bullies to leave him alone. As a last resort, he had to bloody some heads to earn their respect.

Preferring solitude on the trail, he camped far from town and trail. Marshaling worked best when no one knew he was around. He was headed for Ft. Hall as his first stop. The fort was a major resupply stop on the Oregon Trail. Wagons headed north to the Blue Mountains and farther northwest to the Dulles. Settlers resting and resupplying would stop there, to share any news they had.

News was always welcome on the trail. If anyone had experienced trouble or knew of any robberies or murders, this would be the first place he would catch any new events as to what might be going on. The closer he got to Names Hill crossing, the fresher the stories would be. By the time he got to Angelle's, he expected to have a pretty good grasp of the gang's activities. He had not traveled the Greenwood Cutoff, so he wanted to see the conditions on the trail for himself.

Taking up the reins of his packhorse, Shepherd and Dusty set off into the unknown to find what he could find. He had experienced misery and death on the trail, himself. It angered him that men could make a dangerous journey even more dangerous by preying on their own kind. There were times men could be so despicable that he was ashamed of belonging to the human race.

CHAPTER 3

Fort Hall was busy. Shepherd was surprised to see so many pilgrims and travelers. It was late in the year to be this far east. Wagons were stocking up for the winter or for making a last-minute dash across the mountains. It was always a gamble. Stay and eat up your supplies and whatever money you may have, or test your luck against the oncoming winter storms, if your funds were low. Any flip of a coin could result in the same tragedy. There were no guarantees, one way or another.

The Suttler's store would be his best chance to hear gossip, stock up supplies for himself, have a drink, and talk to the locals. It would also give his animals a day or two of rest before continuing.

Shepherd gave his list to the salesman behind the counter. He wanted canned beans, vegetables and fruit, coffee, bacon, jerky, salt, sugar, canned milk, tea, flour, saleratus, and lard. He added a new pair of pants, a flannel shirt, and finally a wool coat. It was getting colder.

"Sorry, we don't serve your kind in here." The clerk threw Shepherd's list back on the counter. "Get out, before I have you thrown out."

"What was that, Mister? I don't think I heard you right." Shepherd leaned over the counter toward the clerk so he could see the man's eyes when he replied.

"I said…"

"What is it, Dennis? Trouble?"

"Tom, I was just telling this fella, we don't serve his kind in here."

"I make those decisions, Dennis. Was he drunk? Is he cussin'? What was wrong?"

"Tom, where I come from, we don't cotton to no Negras."

"Does he have the money? Was he trying to steal from us? Let me look at you, Mister. Lord, have mercy! Dennis, he is black for sure…" Tom started chuckling to himself and looked at Shepherd with a large grin on his face.

"Now see here…I didn't come into this place to be insulted." Shepherd fumed. "Fill my order or there will be hell to pay. I'm a Federal officer."

"Shepherd! Don't ya know me? It's Tom Dearborn. You saved me and my family's lives a few years ago. Dennis, this is one of the finest men I've ever met. I'd be honored to wait on you, Shepherd. What do you want? Dennis, never talk like that again, about any man out here. You don't have any idea who you may be talking with. If Shepherd would have jerked you across that counter and punched your face, I would say you had it coming. Old ways from back east don't count out here in the wilderness. Go wait on somebody else. Friend Shepherd, did you see if those pants fit you right? We got some good plaid wool coats in just last week. Mackinaws is what they call 'em. Let me show them to you."

"Tom. It is good to see you again." He watched Dennis skulk away with a blank look on his face. "I thought you had left the country. When I last saw you, you had had enough and was headed back down the trail. How's the family?"

"We're all fine, Shepherd. After we left, we stopped here for a time to rest and regroup, try to think our plans through. I got a job at the store here. Now, I'm part owner. You know those men who tried to rob us and you and your friends stopped them back on the trail? They showed up here and robbed us. Took the money from the cash box, stole a shirt and hat and a box of cigars. Did you ever see those men again? I hope they got caught. Rotten scoundrels for certain."

"They were caught and killed, Tom. I was there. That whole gang is dead." Shepherd didn't go into details.

"Good riddance, I say. Let's fill this order. How about supper tonight? My wife would be plumb tickled to fix you a good meal. What are you doing out this way? You and that posse were all headed for Salem, weren't you?"

"Salem? Yes, we were as I remember. Supper with your wife's cooking? You can count on me, Tom. I've been on the trail for a long time again. I've got some questions I need to have answers to. Maybe you could help me out."

"I'd like that, Shepherd. Come to the house tonight, we can talk over supper. Let me take care of the rest of your list."

Shepherd pushed his chair back from the table after coffee and a fried dried apple pie and patted his stomach. "Thank you, Mrs. Dearborn, I enjoyed that tremendously. I haven't had a good meal since I left Salem and I like my own cooking."

Tom filled in the rest of Shepherd's questions over another cup of coffee when they were alone. "I've been thinking over what you said, your mission is out on the cutoff. We have had reports of robbery and much worse for about a year. Fortunate people were rescued when another group approached during the robbery, and the robbers took off. They were white men. Sometimes folks reported it was Indians. No one wants to chase them into the desolation, using up water and their stock they would need as they continued their travel west.

The gang seems to be opportunistic. They attack when it is easy prey then vamoose when they are challenged. The Mormon cart pushers don't stand a chance out there. Of course, the ones that were murdered can't speak. Some emigrants ask about fellow travelers, whom they've missed. Most assume they took another trail. We don't hear back once they've left. You can bet something is happening out there. I'm glad the territory is doing something about it. You be careful. Angelle's is not a savory place. Right-thinking men won't let their women step foot inside the doors. You watch how you grind your corn. Don't trust anybody."

"Thanks, Tom, I won't. Sounds like a complicated job. They must have a place they can hole up with water. I wonder…have you noticed individual men spending a lot more money than they used to or someone buying up ranches and land? The assessor's office would be a good place to look."

"What assessor's office, Shepherd? There's nothing out there. No towns, no water."

"Hmm. Somebody has money, you can bet on that. I'll have to sniff them out. Again, Mrs. Dearborn, thank you for a delicious meal. I'm back on the trail in the morning. I'll say good night. Hope to see you on my way back, Tom."

Shepherd realized he had a puzzle to solve. People had been robbed then murdered. Women had been defiled, and no sign of the perpetrators, except arrow-littered bodies and empty, burned wagons. Two-hundred-fifty square miles of featureless scrub desert to search. No one had ridden after the gang. No one knew anything about them. Maybe they were Indians preying on the white invaders. It was easier than having to hunt for your food.

Further complicating his puzzle was the fact that the trail was more a direction than an established path. The area was level with low, rolling hills. Emigrants simply headed toward the direction they thought was best, following their noses instead of a road. Easy pickings for an alert predator. So far, he had a lot of pieces to his puzzle. Hopefully, they would start to form a pattern after a while. He hoped so. People were dying and his job was to stop them, however way he could. Lyle had said to wipe them out.

Travel on the old trail was nostalgic for Shepherd. He was a seasoned veteran, surviving Indian attacks, animal attacks, even gunshot wounds. A man to ride the river with. Approaching trains or individuals eyed him suspiciously, until he flashed his badge. In most cases, he was the first sign of law and order they had seen in hundreds of miles. He was welcomed around campfires, invited to dinner. His skin played no part in the hospitality he was shown. People welcomed him, because he was news. He had traveled the trails He had survived. Eager for word of what came next was uppermost in the minds of most of the travelers. Not knowing what lay in store for them was everyone's biggest concern. What comes next?

Shepherd shared his story of his coming up the Oregon Trail, using it to draw stories in return from the travelers without them knowing he was digging for information. More and more wagons were using the cutoff as it saved them over ten days' travel time. A risk more and more were willing to take as the season grew later into the year. He learned many had seen abandoned wagons and carts, dead animals along the cutoff, evidence of the difficulties of travel with no water and no food for the animals. Some of the dead bodies, folks had assumed died from deprivation or disease. If they had time, they buried the remains; if disease was suspect, they covered them with rocks and brush or let them lie.

The farther Shepherd traveled, more and more pieces were gathered, but no patterns were forming. He knew they would with time.

When he arrived at Names Hill, he could see the expanse of the desert beyond. It was unlike the desert he had travelled, on another adventure searching for his brother, several years earlier. This, was a broad, open, featureless plane, with low-level sagebrush, nothing higher than three feet off the ground growing in all directions. Low-level hills with hidden deep gullies and dry streambeds, a palate of silvers, grays and browns, populated by snakes and jackrabbits. No green painted the picture before him, a telltale sign of water. No water. No life. The Green River was the only green vein of life here. Pilgrims rejoiced to find it. There was a treacherous crossing with a high bank on the west side of the river if you did not get bogged down in the quicksand called Names Hill. In the dry heat of summer, you could walk across it. A few miles farther north was a Mormon ferry, a much safer crossing, but only Mormons crossed for free. They charged everyone else. A little payback for all the offences the brotherhood had suffered on their westward track.

After traversing the desert and reaching Names Hill, exhausted weakened animals pulled the wagons up the sharp incline, strained at the traces, their sides heaving with the effort. Wise travelers stayed for a day to water and feed their stock and let them rest from the dry trip. Less wise pilgrims moved on, paying no heed to their poor stock, only to see them waste away and die. The only benefit to them then was to eat the emaciated creatures, as they lamented their bad fortune and how they might finish the journey.

Shepherd found carcasses and ruined wagons as he approached the hill. He was glad his group had taken extra time and had gone to Bridger's fort on the lower Green River, thereby avoiding the desert cutoff. Four wagons approached the river. Shepherd watched them cross and begin the muscle-wrenching climb up the hill. "Guess, I'll go and make some friends." He urged Dusty down the slope as he shook out a loop.

Chapter 4

—◆◇✦◇◆—

Shepherd started down the slope, waving to the wagons. The drivers paused as he approached. "Ya need a hand getting up this slope? It's pretty damn steep. Name's Shepherd." He threw a loop over a wagon spar and helped pull the wagon up the steep hill.

One by one, each wagon lurched over the rim of Names Hill, leaving everyone exhausted. The women brought some vinegar and water to drink with a little sugar in it. "We ran out of lemon extract weeks ago. Hope to find some more at Fort Hall. Hope you like it. We've become partial to it."

He enjoyed the drink and found it refreshing. With practiced eye, he noted the condition of the stock and the people. These folks drove mules and had taken four days to cross the desert, stocking the wagon with hay and water proven worthwhile. Friends of theirs had turned south, toward Bridger's fort, because they felt the oxen would be too slow, taking at least twice the time. It was late in the year; sacrifices were made for speed and safety.

Bill and Frieda Todd were in their twenties, Shepherd figured, still robust with a veteran look to them. No children or sentiment for furniture or religious doctrine drove them. They were practical, learning the way of the

West as they came. Their dream was Oregon and the new life beckoning with promise. They had come across the cutoff with four other wagons, young people, like themselves.

"We sold our furniture at Angelle's to lighten our load and save our mules. Didn't get much. They charged a month's wages for poor hay and water, but it got us through." Shepherd talked to all four families that evening around the campfire. They had joined up in Independence with a large train moving out. Soon, they saw their sentiments were similar and traveled together, helping and learning from each other and their experienced scout. They were better off taking the cutoff, because they were willing to travel lean and take care of their stock. There would be household goods to buy in Oregon, or they would make their own. They didn't feel the need to bring long-term household goods with them. The rest of the train had split to go to Bridger's fort and winter there. The Todds were going to Fort Hall for the winter with no delusions about crossing the mountains in the winter. Spring would be soon enough to cross. Getting there alive was this group's priority. Shepherd told them to look up Tom Dearborn and place their trust in him at the fort.

"How was the crossing for the cutoff? You look good. Your stock looks good. How did you handle it?"

"We have traveled light since Independence. Just food and provisions for the trail was what we carried. At Angelle's, we bought hay and water. We all carried extra water barrels and added another before we started. He was hard to deal with, that Angelle. Firewood was expensive too. We all went in on the wood and shared it as a group. Kept one fire at night for meals and in the morning, we used only enough to make coffee and a quick hoecake or two. We made time by making a good plan." Bill and the other men agreed.

"How were the trails? There's been reports of robbery

and killing on the cutoff. Weren't you informed of those, before you set off?" Shepherd drank some tea laced with his canned milk and sugar. He liked his tea sweet, coffee too, with canned milk.

"Even though we didn't trust him too much, Angelle did warn us to keep together and keep a wary eye out. 'There be robbers on the trail. Don't trust anybody's.' He told us."

"He did?" Shepherd was impressed. He had visioned Angelle as maybe the leader of this gang, but now he wasn't so sure.

"There were ruined wagons and dead animals to be sure. What puzzled us more than anything were tracks of wagons, just heading off into the desert. There is no place to go out there for water when the Green River is another ten to fifteen miles away. Why would they take such a chance, Mister? You've been on the trail. Why go off in such a way?"

"Did the tracks all go off in any one direction?" Shepherd was thoughtful. This was what he was trying to find out.

"Seemed to all go off to the north, on the east side of the trail." They all agreed.

"I'll pass the word with other pilgrims about how you all did. It's good to know some folks has still got common sense." Shepherd bid his friends farewell. He wanted to visit the Mormon ferry, before nightfall.

CHAPTER 5

———————✦———————

"Halt. Be ye a brethren of the Prophet?" A stern-faced man with a full beard but no mustache challenged him as he approached the ferry. "If ye be a brethren, ye are free to pass, if not, wagons are a dollar and horses and rider, fifty cents." Two other men with rifles studied him with no welcoming smiles.

"I am not of the brethren and I will gladly pay for the ferry." Shepherd held out the money. He wanted no trouble. He knew the Mormons had had unfair treatment across the trail. No one wanted them. They were going to their own place in Utah. Their own state if they could make it happen. He had no corn to grind with them that was for sure.

"I came west, brother. All the way to Independence. Me and my pa. I owe them my life. I am glad to pay. Perhaps you would help me?"

"Help you? What would you require from us?"

"Information, brother, information is all. May I speak with the elder of your group? I am peaceful. My intent is only to help if I can."

"Stay where you are. Stephan, inform Elder Jebidiah."

"Leave your guns and come with me. What is your name?"

"I am Shepherd. I assure you I am peaceful. I represent

the law in this Territory." He flipped his lapel to reveal his badge.

"We have had little peace with anyone representing the law in this country or any other part of the country. Leave your weapons or go on your way."

"Alright, alright. I understand." Shepherd left his guns with his horse and pack animal and followed the man a short distance to some wagons pulled together around a common fire.

"This man is called Shepherd. He asked to speak to our elder. Says he is a federal marshal."

Elder Jebidiah was sitting in willow chair with a blanket over his lap. He was holding a cup of tea in both hands as if to warm them. "Yes." He nodded to the first man.

"He is called Shepherd."

The elder paused for a brief time, pondering the name. "What do you want, Shepherd?"

"I would like to show you my badge. I am a territorial deputy investigating robberies and murder on the Greenwood Cutoff. I'd like to ask a few questions of you, if I may?"

"Deputy marshal! You a Negro deputy marshal?" Elder Jebidiah burst into deep laughter until he had to wipe the tears from his eyes.

Shepherd stepped back. He was embarrassed and turned to leave.

"Please forgive me, Shepherd, but your statement was so unexpected, I couldn't believe it. Then when you showed your badge, I could only envision the expression on some white slave owner's face. I would pay a gold sovereign to have seen it just once. He, he, he," he laughed. "Please sit down. Bring Deputy Shepherd a cup of tea. You drink tea, Shepherd?"

"I do."

"Sit. Tell me what you want to ask."

Shepherd explained his mission to the elder. Elder Jebidiah told him of several episodes of Mormon hand-carters they had been told were robbed and left on the trail with nothing. Any show of resistance meant a bullet. Elder Jebidiah knew of five deaths reported to him in the last year alone. Murdered and brutalized. Some tortured and burned.

"They don't bother us here. We're too strong, but on the trail, anyone alone means almost certain death. We have urged all brethren to stay together in groups of ten or more when they make the crossing. It takes fifteen good days of travel by foot. It is difficult to carry enough water, let alone food for that kind of dry crossing. Few attempt it."

"Thank you, Elder. That is what I needed to know. Any characteristic about the gang you can tell me so I can identify them?"

"Nothing that I can tell you. They all are pretty common men, nothing distinguishing about them that anyone reported. One was a shorter man than the rest. They are not Indians that is certain. They are white men."

CHAPTER 6

———— ◆ ◂◈▸ ◆ ————

S hepherd had a lot to think about before he headed into the desert. He watered and fed Dusty and his pack animal well with grain and green hay, purchased from the brethren. They could only carry so much in lieu of his other provisions.

He found it eerie in the desert as daylight began to break. No landmarks. No tree or hillsides. Silence hung over him as a thick blanket of omnipresence. Dew on the sagebrush moistened Dusty's legs, kicking water up on Shepherd's pants and boots as they pushed through the thick brush. The feral smell of the sagebrush and the morning damp reminded him of burning rotted wood for some strange reason. Sound carried for long distances. He heard wagons approaching, before he could see them rising out of the desert like masts of ships on the horizon. It would be easy to lose your way. If the sky was cloudy and you lost your direction, you could make a wrong turn. Your team could wander off the trail and you might not even know it.

He understood that travelers were wary of him. He waved and approached two wagons traveling together. Both kept a shotgun poised toward him at all times as he rode up to them.

"Hey, I'm friendly." He held up his right hand with his badge displayed and most importantly, a broad friendly smile. It bought good will.

At ease, the emigrants answered his questions. No, they hadn't had any trouble. No, they hadn't seen anyone else on the trail. Shepherd pointed the right direction to them and showed them his trail, if they doubted his word. A piece of cake wrapped in a kerchief was thrust in his hand at one wagon by a grateful woman. Seeing another friendly human being seemed to encourage them to go on. He bit into the cake as he rode away, a smile on his face. That would make this trip worthwhile, meeting folks like that, he felt. Stimulated to the job before him, he planned four or five days in the desert at most, as he wanted to get a feel for the place.

The tracks fanned out from all directions as there was no central trail. Here and there were pieces of furniture, dropped and forgotten. Animal bones of poor creatures who simply died of exhaustion and dropped in their traces. He made fires in the morning from sagebrush he had cut the night before and kept covered at night so the morning damp did not affect it. A quick coffee, bacon, and bannock, and he was off traveling in the early hours to spare his stock, as the heat of the day was omnipresent; then it rapidly cooled off. He searched for fires at night, for any campfires glowing against the sky, but saw none.

The third day, a track ventured off to the north. His curiosity aroused, he followed for a few miles making sure he marked his trail as he went. About a mile into the track, the land dipped into several descending swales. This desert was not as flat as it looked. At the bottom was a burned handcart, with open bags and chests. Two bodies riddled with arrows were draped over the remains of the cart.

The smoky, burned cart was a charred heap. The clothing of the victims wasn't burnt, so they were shot after the cart was set on fire and it went out. Shepherd mused as he rode slowly around the scene. Standing in his stirrups, he glanced around the area to be sure no one was about, before sliding off of Dusty to examine the scene further. The woman's arms were tied and her skirts and apron were torn from her. Shepherd only glanced at the poor woman for a brief second, before turning away in revulsion.

"Whoever did this were animals," he fumed. Then anger came flooding up through his body in heaving waves, causing him to lose his breakfast while he kneeled in the drying sagebrush, gasping for breath and control of himself. He buried them with much respect under stones and sagebrush. There was no shovel in the cart. Animals had not violated the bodies yet, not even the vultures that were circling overhead. This was a recent event, happening in the last forty-eight hours.

Thick sagebrush made it difficult to find tracks, but Shepherd found broken stems and places where the sage had yielded to pressure, as horses passed pointing the direction of travel from four riders. He followed. Whoever they were, they didn't try to cover their tracks. They weren't worried about anyone following them.

Cautiously, he followed a descending gradient for another two miles, until it butted up against a steep cut in the hillside about twenty feet high. Here, the tracks ended on the bedrock beneath the cut. Shepherd found no sign going either to the right or the left. He added another piece of this puzzle to those floating in his head, nothing coming together yet. He did have a glimpse of the personality of this gang. They were cold-blooded killers, if ever he had seen one.

Returning to the trail, Shepherd continued east. They would be thirsty by the time they got to Angelle's on the banks of the Big Sandy. He should be there tomorrow. If memory served him well, the Big Sandy was not much more than a shallow stream you could step across. Bitter determination gripped him. Lyle's words played over and over in his mind. "Wipe them out. Wipe them out."

Angelle's store appeared as expected as he looked across the river. From the top of the limestone ridge, he observed a squat log building with a low porch across the front. A corral at the far end and then a ramshackle barn. Crude shingles topped the store's log walls sunburned to a dirty gray patina. A carved six-foot-tall statue of a beautiful angel, garishly painted red with golden wings adorned the crown of the roof. Furniture of every description littered the yard, providing shade and perches for the several dozen chickens nesting in drawers and empty butter churns. Cats and dogs loitered beneath the wooden porch. A hitching rail stood next to a murky watering trough where a multicolored cock crowed loudly while stretching its wings and defecating into the trough. A sign written with a clumsy hand in red paint proclaimed ANGELLE'S LAST STOP hung under the porch roof. Double wooden louvered doors marked the entrance.

Angelle's sat on the eastern inhospitable banks of the Big Sandy River. Only rocks and sand decorated the landscape. The last stop for water and supplies, before crossing the fifty miles of the Sublette Cutoff rose out of the desert like a sick apparition of despair and ruin. It's only saving grace was the trickle of water admirably called a river. Faded silver-gray signs tacked to the wall fronts read, *Supplies, Last water for 60 miles, Fodder for Animals, Good prices, ALL WELCOME*. Signs painted in red to match the painted red of the angel on the roof. Two horses and a pack mule stood slack-legged at the rail, swishing flies with bristly tails, heads down sniffing at dogs out of boredom.

The flashy rooster jumped up on the edge of the trough and crowed. Large piles of firewood were spilled off to one

side in a pile and water barrels were stacked close to a
bridge over the river. He approached a sign on the side of
the bridge. It read: *Toll Bridge, wagons $1.00.
Horses/Mules/Ox 50 cts, Man or Woman, $1.00, All others
.25 cents.* The bridge was no more than twenty feet across.
A team of four mules would be over the other side before a
wagon would be completely on the bridge. At best, the
water was ankle deep. You could ford the stream a few feet
away, except for the fact the western side of the river was a
steep fifteen-foot embankment of boulders topped by a
solid ridge of limestone that ran for miles along the west
side of the river.

Angelle had blasted their embankment down to be
level with the streambed. It was the only easy ford for miles
in any direction.

"Seems to me, this Angelle is making a mint. He's got
everything covered." Shepherd chuckled to Dusty and
approached the bridge.

"Can you read, Mister?"

"Yes, I can."

"It's 75 cents for the horse and you. You got the coin
or you can jump off of the bank, over there." A big fellow
sitting under an umbrella next to a boulder motioned to the
limestone edge of the river with his shotgun.

"Do I ride, or do I walk across?" Shepherd flipped
three coins to the man.

"Makes no difference to me. We charge for everything
that crosses, horses and wagons, men and niggers."

Shepherd stared at the fat man as he rode over the
bridge, from beneath the brim of his hat. This was not the
time to draw any more attention to himself, so he kept his
mouth shut. He tipped his hat to the guard on the other side
of the bridge. "I paid once, do I have to pay when I go
back?"

"Yep. Go or stay. Makes no difference. You pays your
money when you use the bridge comin' and goin'."

"Thought so." Shepherd crossed the bridge and pulled up at the hitching rail in front of the store. The two horses and pack mule remained as before. Shepherd took his animals to water at the trough. They welcomed the murky green stuff, sucking greedily on the algae-ridden water. Shepherd decided to try his luck and the water and whiskey inside.

There were windows on both sides of the room. A bar at the far end and store goods at the other.

"Let me have a whiskey and a glass of water, please." Shepherd tugged at his gloves, laid them on the counter, and reached into his pocket for the money. A poker game next to Shepherd got up from the table and moved to the back of the room. Another man chose to move to the end of the bar.

"We don't serve niggers, Mister. Get your whiskey someplace else."

"You know, I've been hearing that more and more recently." Shepherd pulled his gun and pointed it at the bartender's chest. "Do I look like a nigger to you? Some people have been mixing me up with somebody else. Do I look like a nigger to you?"

The bartender bent to reach under the bar for a gun. Shepherd leaned over and grabbed him by the collar, pulling him over the bar. Then he pushed the side of his face flat on the bar with one hand and placed his Patterson's barrel pointed to his nose with the other hand.

"Can you see the chambers in my revolver? Is it loaded?"

The man's snaky eyes now bulged, fixed on the chambers of Shepherd's gun. He tried to nod his head. Shepherd thumped his head on the bar.

"Is it loaded?"

"A—a yes," he croaked.

"Then possibly... You have to allow, it's possible that you have me mixed up with someone else's nigger. Is that possible?"

"Yeah…yeah…sure. Sure. It's possible."

"I will have a glass of water and a whiskey, please." Shepherd picked up the Patterson next to the man's face and released him. "I wouldn't want to kill a man, just because he couldn't tell one nigger from another. I'll have my drinks over there." Shepherd pointed to a table next to the fireplace. He sat down and put his feet up on a chair sitting sideways to the fire, with his back to the wall. The bartender quickly filled the glasses and brought them to the table.

"Here's your drinks." The bartender sat them down. "That's two dollars for the drinks."

"Two dollars!" exclaimed Shepherd. "How much is your whiskey?"

"Whiskey is two bits. Water is six bits."

Shepherd nodded with understanding dawning in his mind. "Whiskey is two bits, water is a buck and a half." He handed two one-dollar bills to the bartender. "Keep the change."

The bartender looked at the two greenbacks in his hand, started to turn back, stopped, and retreated behind the bar.

Shepherd sniffed his water, sipped it, and then drank half the glass down, smacking his lips. Not bad.

Phineas' encounter had refined him somewhat. Now his habit, he sniffed the whiskey, sipped, and then swallowed half the glass, enjoying the burn going down. At least, Angelle's sold straight up whiskey.

A large shadow passed over him. He looked up to see an enormous man, the biggest man Shepherd had ever seen. *He must weigh over four hundred pounds and stand six foot, six inches at least.*

The huge, dark-haired man with a crooked, smashed nose was talking to the bartender. Shepherd heard whispers. "Drink, nigger, gun, misunderstanding, shoot…" Turning his massive head to look at him, the big man sized him up in a glance, pulled a coin out of his pocket, and tossed it in the air, catching it as it fell. He slapped it on the bar, muttered, "U huh." In three steps, he was on top of Shepherd, grabbing him by both shoulders. "Who is you, Mister?"

"I am Shepherd McKinzey," he squeaked and struggled to his feet then shrugged off the man's hands and hit the man full on the bottom of his chin with both fists in a double uppercut. The man didn't move, except to stare at him. His eyes bore down on Shepherd, then the monster grabbed him by the neck, lifted him up off of his feet. Bringing Shepherd close to his face, he hissed, "Who is you, really?" The grip on his throat lessened so he could speak.

"I'm a United States Deputy Marshal, Shepherd McKinzey. Who, who are you?' he croaked, sucking in what little air he could.

"Da hell you say." The giant released Shepherd, dropping him back in his chair. "I'm Da'vid Angelle, I own dis place. We don tink to much of your kind down in Louisian'. What chou want here?" He leaned over to the side of Shepherd's neck, as if to threaten him eye to eye. In a whispered voice, he said, "Play alon wit me. I explain later." Then standing to his full height and glowering at Shepherd. In a loud voice he said, "Finish yor drink and git out. We don't abide your kind, no matter whats dey call themselves."

A confused Shepherd leaned back in his chair and sipped on his water. "Most expensive water I've ever had. I think I will take my time and enjoy it." He smiled and pushed his hat back on his head as he slid down in his chair.

Da'vid closed on him before the smile left his face, grabbed Shepherd out of his chair, and pulled him close. "Play alon wit me, like I say. Meet me out by da corral at nightfall," he murmured under his breath, before shaking the marshal like a rag doll and throwing him back into his seat. "You paid for it. Drink it and get out." He stormed out of the room like a breathing thunderstorm, shaking the floor as he went, tossing chairs and tables out of his way. The giant stopped and turned to the bartender. "If he be hare in ten minutes, shoot him." Da'vid turned to go then turned back. "Don't get the floor bloody, I jus' mopped it. Shoot him outside." The rest of the patrons cast annoyed looks at Shepherd and went back to their drinking.

Shepherd gulped his whiskey, started to leave, picked up his water, and drank that down. "I'm going. I'm going. Just wanted a drink and some water. I'm going."

The bartender clutched a Sharpe's rifle in his hand and stepped from behind the bar. "I'll mess you up good, if'n you don't get out of here."

"I'm gone, Mister." Shepherd made it out the door and mounted Dusty, his mind reeling. He kicked his horse like he was terrified and galloped away. "What the hell is going on here?" He headed east away from Angelle's toward the old Oregon Trail, not wanting to give these crazy people any more of his money, but most importantly, he wanted to leave behind the image of a scared man running.

CHAPTER 7

———— ◦•◈•◦ ————

Shepherd made camp in a dry wash several miles from Angelle's. He lashed the branches of some mesquite trees together and threw a blanket over them to give him some shade, then he laid down and took a nap until evening. *What is this all about? Meet him by the corral after dark? Am I crazy? Is he going to kill me?* More and more pieces kept jumbling around in his head, but he was seriously curious. "I just got to know what he wants."

An hour before nightfall, Shepherd crept within five hundred feet of the store. He wanted a good view to see if he was being set up. No one appeared. Other than a few stragglers riding in and out, nothing moved. No wagons came in. No one he recognized from inside the building left. All was quiet except the cock on the water trough crowing to the sun as it was setting.

Moving to a spot where he was shielded by thick sagebrush, Shepherd waited. The two bridge guards came in before dusk, leaving no lookouts he could spot. Shepherd moved closer to the corral.

A door banged and a big voice called, "come here' ma burros. Come eat, ma babies." Angelle moved about the corral walking with a bucket of feed. "Come Cher, I feed you good."

Shepherd crept nearer staying under cover but within earshot. No one else was in sight.

"Yo her' Marshal? Clear your throat if you are. Don' show yo' self."

Shepherd cleared his throat as instructed.

"Listen ta me. I is glad yo is come. Dings are no good here. Dat's it ma babies, eat your food." The big man sat his bucket down and leaned against the top rail of the corral, rolling a cigarette. He spoke to Shepherd in a low voice so only he could hear. "Bad men got control of ma place. They wait for da poor folks ta come and rob and kill dem in the wasteland. The two men who guard da bridge is some of dem. Dare's lots more, maybe six or seven hiding in da desert. They kill me if I don' go along. They hurt everybody. If yo a genuine marshal like you say, stay hidden, don' let dem know yo is around. They kill you sure."

Louder, he called out, "Dat's it, Martha, don' let Clem dare took your food. I scratch yo ears. Yo like dat." He lowered his voice. "Hide out, watch dis place, follow da next wagons and see what happens ta dem. Maybe you can do somding. I don't know what. Take a burro or two if'n you wan', so's you can hide out. Dares water bags on the side of da barn. Help yoself, just don' get caught. It be the las I ever saw of ya. I feed da burros every night, dis time. Come if ya can. I try to help. Gotta go. They watch me. Enoff, Enoff, Martha, yo a pig." Angelle emptied his bucket in the trough, patting each burro as he passed. "I leave supplies for ya by dis fence at night. Der's hay in barn. They won' know yo took none."

"Hey, Angelle. What are you doing, get your fat ass in here. Your grub is burning on the stove!"

Angelle dropped his bucket to his side. "Be careful, Mr. Marshal." He hurriedly made his way to the store. "I's commin'. Don't none of ya kno how ta lift a pan of tators off of de stove?"

"Who you talkin' too out there anyway?"

"I talk ta ma damn burros. Dey is da only dings that listen to ol' Angelle, des days." The door slammed shut with a loud bang.

The silence in the desert could be very loud. Shepherd sat back on his haunches pondering Da'vid Angelle's words in stunned profundity. *Was he telling the truth?* Pieces were starting to join up with other pieces.

He crept to the barn looking for the water bags and anything else he might need. He found them where he had been told, scooped up some oats and corn for his horses, stumbled over an old set of panniers buried under the hay pile. After stuffing them with hay, he crept back to Dusty, before they slipped back to their hidden campsite without being seen. He kept a cold camp that night and wished he'd brought another blanket.

Firelight travels far in the desert night; he wouldn't chance it. Someone, somewhere, might spot it. Angelle had warned him, they were killers. Cold bannock and jerky for another night, though he treated himself to a can of applesauce and buried the can in the sand. Tomorrow, he would start his vigilance, watching for movement of the gang at the store and waiting for wagons to come into the baited trap of Angelle's store and café with the beautiful angel beckoning to wayward travelers.

CHAPTER 8

———◆◆◆◆◆———

Next morning, Shepherd scouted along the riverbank. He needed to be able to cross without going over the bridge. There had to be some break in the stone shelf that was large enough, he, Dusty, and the pack animal could get through.

It was early fall. The air was dry. Nights were getting colder. Moisture got sucked up into the greedy air, no matter the temperature. He would need a place to camp where he could have a fire without being seen.

A jackrabbit darted out from the tumbleweeds next to Dusty's feet, startling both horse and rider.

"Whoa, Dusty, whoa. Just a rabbit. Where did he go?" Shepherd searched the ground for tracks. The rabbit had gone off to his left toward the river. He turned Dusty left on a hunch, following the rabbit. All animals have to drink. They found a well-used trail, trod by many feet; rabbit, goat, coyote, skunk all followed same path to the river, going and coming. Antelope tracks piqued his interest the most.

Shepherd slid out of his saddle and led Dusty forward to the bank of the river. Nothing stood out to him on the other side. It appeared to be an impenetrable shelf of rock. There was no passage through the opposite bank, unless you were a mountain sheep. He hunted along the riverbank on his right, pushing through thick dead brush and small broken stumps.

At first, it looked like the rest of the stone bank, where the river turned sharply east, but Shepherd spied tracks on the other side of the water over a slab of rock jutting out of the bank. A single trail of prints led up to the stone face and disappeared.

Ground hitching Dusty, he waded the river to see where the tracks led. A crack in the rock face solved his dilemma. It appeared animals passed behind the front rock façade climbing up a narrow, steep open chute to the top. The rocks were broken due to some high-pressure ridge that had fractured them, eons ago.

With a little muscle power, Shepherd was able to clear loose rocks and boulders he could lift out of the way, making a wide enough trail for his horses to pass. He could understand why no one had discovered this before.

From ten feet away, you could not tell there was an entrance here wide enough for a horse. Shepherd piled the rocks on top of the rock shelf in such a way to look random, but in a pattern only he would recognize.

Leading his animals around and through then up the sharp incline took some time. His pack animal scrambled up the narrow path following Dusty, sides heaving as he struggled to keep his feet in the loose rock, but soon they were on top of level rock looking over the river. Shepherd brushed out their prints in the riverbank with a branch and threw water over them allowing the imprints to melt back into the sand, appearing flat and unmarred.

Now to find a camp and a place to watch the outpost. He could follow any stray wagon that came to the store from this side and watch the activity from an obscure hiding spot. With the extra feed and water bags, Shepherd felt he could hole up for four to five days if need be, before he had to resupply.

The landscape was deceiving, a seemingly flat level plain that rolled and dipped, sometimes into deep narrow ravines created by pressure ridges running through the rock table. He had to be careful as the sagebrush and tumble weeds covered everything, obscuring loose rocks and deep fissures that could twist an ankle, break a leg, or hide a rattler.

Shepherd let Dusty have his head, guiding him with his knees as he searched for a hiding spot in the rough terrain. He followed the pressure ridge from the river north until he found a suitable open crack he could hide in safely.

The pressure ridge had lifted a slab of the rock ridge, forming a declivity in the landscape wide and deep enough to form a dugout. Rain had washed the soil away from under the slab, leaving a triangle-shaped cut covered with thick sagebrush. There was room for all of them. A fire would be well hidden and any smoke dissipated by the overlying sage. As long as they didn't have any downpours, he would have a dry place to stay hidden.

Shepherd left what he had taken from Angelle's in his dugout then sought his temporary camp of the night before, returning with the rest of his supplies. Once he got his settled, he went in search of an observation site to watch the trading post.

He established a lookout, a few hundred yards north and east of the store. From here, he could view the road and the storefront. It was midmorning and Shepherd sat back to watch with his field glasses in his hands. So far everything was coming together; puzzle pieces still swirled in his head. Soon he knew they would fall into place. He had to be patient. He had to be alert. *These rattlesnakes do not rattle.*

There were no wagons or emigrants that day. Several riders came and went. The bridge guards were changed. That meant neither of the new ones had seen him before.

Dusk began to fall and he made his way back to Angelle's.

Angelle came out like the night before with a bucket of feed in his hands and a sack over his shoulder. "Yo here?"

Shepherd coughed.

The big man fondled his furry charges, stroked their ears, petted them, cooing how much he loved them, and dumped the cloth sack of food over the rail to Shepherd.

A man came out of the back door, stared over to the corral for a minute, and then went back inside. Angelle talked to his wards, hand- feeding them, paying no attention to the man on the porch. After the door slammed shut, he watched to see if anyone else came out. Silently, he opened the gate and pushed a lone burro out, looking around to see if anyone watched him. "Took him, no one will miss hit."

The burro simply stood where he was like he was waiting to be led away. After Angelle went back inside, Shepherd crawled over and grabbed the burro's bridle and led it away through the sagebrush without making a sound. He filled the water bags at the crossing, loaded up the burro, and headed back to his hole in the ground.

Shepherd fashioned a stove from flat rocks scattered around the cut. One reason was to keep his fire hidden as much as possible; another was to warm the rocks to act as a heat source. It was getting colder at night. Burning old dried sagebrush made a quick, hot burning fire that did not throw off a bunch of smoke yet heated the slabs of his rock stove, creating a radiant heat that lasted for hours. Going to bed that night, he wrapped several heated rocks in his blankets and kept warm, until he changed them out later for other hot rocks when he restoked the fire.

He always woke about two in the morning for his call to the bushes. He also checked the stock, fired up the stove again, and wrapped up rocks still hot from the earlier fire to warm him for the rest of the night. He slept fitfully. Tomorrow, he would close off the ends of his cave to block the wind more.

For two more days, he stayed low, listening and watching. No wagons came to the store. At night, he would fill his water skins and steal hay from the barn, stockpiling some for when he might not be able to do this safely. He did not visit Angelle again. The burro came in very handy for hauling water and hay as he made very little noise and was small enough to be unnoticeable moving through the brush.

Shepherd liked the little fellow, for he followed him wherever he went. He rubbed his head and ears. "You got to stay here, sorry." He apologized to him while he tethered him between Dusty and the packhorse in their hideout. He decided to continue to watch a few more days. If no emigrants came, he would have to change his plan and start scouting deeper into the desert looking for any other sign of activity by the gang or their hideout.

"I hope it's not too late in the year," Shepherd said to himself from his lookout perch. "Wagons will stop moving before too long. They'll have to winter over, either at Bridger's fort or Ft. Hall. No chance of crossing the mountains this late."

He watched riders come and go, usually three or four at a time. They would hang around for several hours before fading back into the wilderness. Shepherd was tempted to follow them but stayed on as he didn't want to miss any pilgrims coming through. His first job was to save lives.

One of the riders at the station caught his attention. He was a short, skinny man wearing shiny black boots, a black and silver decorated belt, and rode a horse with a silver saddle. His clothes were new and the other men demurred to him, taking orders when he spoke. Shepherd couldn't hear him, but it was obvious enough. This little man was the boss.

Two more days of watching, and Shepherd was getting impatient. Maybe he would have to change his plans. He learned the character of the men in the gang. The man in black was surely the boss and vainly rode roughshod over the others. Shepherd named him Shorty. He hadn't heard his name called.

Several other men appeared to be his lieutenants, carrying out orders. Angelle was seemingly bossed around. He would argue back, until, the man he decided to call Shorty, who would go and talk with him, then reluctantly the giant would go about his duties. Angelle would occasionally look off in the distance as if he were looking for someone.

CHAPTER 9

A clanging and rattling of chains caught Shepherd's attention midmorning. He could hear them before he could see them. Two wagons came up the trail pulled by mules, small plumes of dust played in swirls of wind each time their hooves struck the stony ground. A barebacked horse was tied to the back of each wagon. Drovers walked along side, cracking their whips and whistling for them to move on. Shepherd moved within earshot.

Shepherd saw Shorty motion for a rider to take off as the wagons pulled in. The rider galloped by them, waving his hat and whooping.

"What's he so happy about?" asked the first drover as Shorty waved him over to the front of the store.

"Going home to his family, I suppose," replied Shorty. "Goin' far? What do you need? We can supply you everything you want to get through the cutoff. You folks is traveling together, I see."

"That's right. We heard about this shortcut. Supposed to be dry with no grass to speak of. What do you suggest we best outfit ourselves with?"

Angelle came out of the store wiping his hands on a towel and tried to get down the steps to the wagons. Two of the lieutenants stopped him before he could get anyone's attention.

Shepherd saw them, brandishing guns, keeping him from talking to the pilgrims. They forced him back inside. "Damn, I hope they don't hurt him," he mumbled to himself. He had grown to admire the big lug.

Shorty kept up a lively patter so the pilgrims would not catch what was going on the porch. "Let me look you over so's I can tell you what you might need. Howdy, ma'am." Shorty touched his hat brim and smiled at the woman sitting on the high seat, before walking along the wagons. "Mind if I look inside?" he asked the drover. "Oh, didn't mean to be standoffish. My name is Lonnie. What's yours?"

So Shorty is Lonnie.

"Mine's Erme." The young drover offered his hand. "Fellow behind us is Coby. Go ahead, we surely could use your advice." Coby came up, and the two pilgrims stood conversing with each other.

Shepherd watched Lonnie say hello to the women and children, smiling and tipping his hat as he opened the back of each wagon looking at their goods. Finished, he rubbed his hands together and approached the two young men.

"Eight mules, seven people, six days if you push it, better count on seven days. Mules is faster than oxen, who would have taken maybe eight days. I think you need to add two more barrels for water on each of your wagons. The ladies won't like it, but you need to dump most of your furniture and put in a load of hay. Unless your mules eat sagebrush and tumbleweed, there is very little grass in those eight days and little else for them to eat."

Erme objected, "No grass at all?"

"You didn't see any cattle as you came through, did you? This country won't even support goats. There is no other water between here and Names Hill, where you will cross the Green River putting you back on the main trail to

Ft. Hall."

Lonnie took off his hat and wiped his face with a neckerchief. "There it is gentlemen, short and not so sweet. I also recommend you buy firewood to cook with. Sagebrush burns hot and fast but it's not good to make a decent fire with, not to cook up a mess of beans or anything but quick cookin'. You need food for yourselves for those eight days. Canned food and jerky is what I recommend, maybe canned milk for your kids, coffee, tea for the adults. You want to keep moving in that desert. It's pretty unforgiving." Shepherd could see, Lonnie was a good salesman.

"The good point is that it will save you another ten days of travel time if'n you had chosen to go to Ft. Bridger. Winter storms is a coming. If you're lucky, you'll make Ft. Hall in two weeks after you cross the Green. Don't loiter long anywhere or you'll be snowed in. My men can help you load your wagons, if'n y'all you want. We're always ready to help pilgrims in need."

Shepherd watched from his vantage point behind a corner of the barn. He couldn't get closer without giving his position away. At least he could hear what Lonnie said to them. It was obvious, the emigrants wanted to get moving. Men scurried about. The women argued, shouting at their husbands, as Lonnie's men unloaded furniture out of the back of both wagons and replaced it with hay and firewood. Water barrels were fitted. Food was brought and loaded into the wagons.

Lonnie presented a bill to the man named Erme.

"What! This is outrageous, Mister. We won't pay this. This is robbery." Erme was in Lonnie's face, waving the bill in front of his nose.

"Gentlemen, gentlemen, what you don't see is the cost of running an establishment like this, clear out in the wilderness. Of course, it's expensive. It's expensive to operate out here, the last vestige of civilization for the next hundred and fifty miles. What did you expect? I have men to pay, supplies to bring in for you, the weary traveler. My costs are exorbitant too. What do you want to put back? The water? Feed for your animals? Food for your family? Tell me. I'll have my men unload it."

Lonnie was polite. He smiled. He was sympathetic. He had them over a barrel and they knew it. Lonnie motioned for his men to start unloading.

Shepherd despised the scene playing out in front of him, but he couldn't make his move , yet. He bit his tongue.

"Wait." Erme frowned and motioned with his hand for Coby to come over. The two young men conferred, and separated to go to their respective wagons, returning with the price Lonnie demanded.

"What about my furniture? Are you going to pay for that?" one of the women demanded.

"Ma'Am." smiled Lonnie as he tipped his hat. "You may take it with you. I have more than I can use." He swept his arm over the yard and all the crumbling furniture strewn about the ground.. She sat down defeated.

The little band set out, only to be stopped at the toll bridge where another loud argument ensued. The guard raised his shotgun and the men shut up, paid the toll, and charged over the bridge and through the gap in the boulder wall.

Shepherd sagged back against the wall of the building shaking his head. "Got 'em coming and going don't you, little man." Reluctantly, he had to give this pack of thieves' credit.

"I suspect you'll see Lonnie's gang after nightfall, is my guess," said Shepherd to himself, as the wagons kicked up dust and rock, scurrying away from the skinning they just got at Angelle's.

CHAPTER 10

S hepherd kept out of sight as he followed the wagons
into the wilderness. They made good time moving
along briskly for the first hour or so. The wagons
stopped to water their mules using the precious supply in
their barrels, when they stopped for a noonin' midday meal.
They continued shortly, wanting to put as much distance
from Angelle's as they could. Making ten miles the first
day, they stopped as dusk was setting in.

The raid came after the mules were unhitched and put
to feed and the supper fire was lit. From the north, calls and
yips could be heard before anything could be seen. Blood
curdling screams and chants terrified the emigrants from all
points around the lone wagons.

"Trying to scare them to death, before they make their
play," Shepherd observed as the scene in front of him
unfolded. He dismounted, leaving Dusty in a safe place,
and moved in a little closer to the brave band and waited.

Erme kicked out the fire, settling the prairie in odd
illumination from a silvery half-moon. Shadows crept near.
Horses whinnied and snorted in the blackness. Sagebrush
snapped as the marauders crept closer.

"Indians, Coby! Keep alert." The two men and their
women gathered their children and dove under their

wagons. The yips began again, with an occasional gunshot shattering the sides of the wagons. The muzzle flashes gave only brief glimpses of how close the attackers were. It was obvious they were outnumbered. Eerie darkness settled over the scene, stimulating imagination and building fear.

"Daddy, I'm scared."

"It's all right, Missy, I'll protect you." Coby put his arm around his daughter's shoulders pulling her close to him. "Now go over to your mama. She needs you to be strong for her." He helped his daughter find her mother's arms then aimed at a movement and fired. "Damn, I cain't see nothin'."

Arrows struck the sides of the wagons, splintering wood and striking panic, as the next wave of the assault began. Return fire from rifles beneath the wagons hit no one. No target had appeared as of yet, only faceless shadows and imagined savages creeping through the brush.

"They're getting closer." Shepherd crawled nearer to the wagons, keeping his distance a little north of the group. Wind blew canvass tops to flapping, sounding like strange birds in the night. He stayed behind their line of fire. "I don't want to be shot by the young men any more than from Shorty's gang." The ambush was also from the north, so he was south of the gang on their left flank. They wouldn't expect an attack from that direction.

Voices muttered within earshot of him, causing him to hug the ground even more.

"He, he, he, Russel, we got those kids buffaloed. They don't know whether to crap or run."

"I know. I can't wait to see how much is in those wagons. Them boys caved pretty quick, when that Lonnie told 'em what they had to pay back at Angelle's. Didn't take long to fork over the cash. I'll bet cha there's lots more."

Some of the gang, I haven't seen yet. Their voices are not familiar, Shepherd surmised, laying down his rifle. He pulled out his pistol and cocked it.

"Did ya hear that, Russel? I thought I heard a gun cocked."

"Lay back down here, Browney. Git your head down. You're edgy, knowing they's women over there. They ain't give the signal yet."

"Well, I thought…" A faint glow lit up in the distance appearing like an evil omen as it was waved over someone's head.

"There it is, Jess. Jesus jist struck a shuck. Les go." Both men started firing at the wagons, scrambling to their feet, passing Shepherd in their eagerness.

"Hands up, boys," Shepherd ordered as he stood to confront the men. Browney turned, dropping to one knee, and opened fire.

Shepherd flung himself to his left, shooting as he went.

"Russel, I'm hit."

"Hol' on, Browney, I'm comin'."

Shepherd shot Russel in the chest. Browney fired back in Shepherd's direction, and Shepherd fanned his gun into the muzzle blast.

"Who the hell ar…" were Jesse's last words.

The men at the wagons were holding their own, firing at the bursts of gunfire from the gang. Shepherd found his rifle and did the same, returning fire toward any gun blast he could see. He was rewarded with a shrill yelp.

"Who's that?'

"Where'd that come from?"

"Browney, is that you?"

"Russel?" Calls from the gang came out of the darkness.

Shepherd blasted away at the voices.

"Let's get outta here!"

"Too many for me."

"I'm cuttin' out, boys."

"Heading back to camp. Got shot in my arm. I'm bleeding."

Horses galloped away in the night, leaving a deafening silence behind.

"No heroes in that bunch." Shepherd listened as the cowardly band tore a hole in the night making their getaway. "I should be able to track them with no problem." He knelt and built a small rock cairn by the side of the trail to mark the spot so he could find it. Steps cracked through the sagebrush behind him.

"Hold it. Put your hands up, Mister, and stand up carefully. Who are you?" The two young men warily approached Shepherd's back, one on each side. "I don't want to shoot you if I don't gotta, but I've been tricked enough and it won't happen again. Thanks for the help, but how did you get here?"

Shepherd held his hands up in the air over his head. "I'm the law. I've been looking for these cutthroats for over a month. Can I put my hands down? I need to examine the men I shot for any information they may have." Shepherd looked over his shoulder at the nervous young men and the double-barreled shotgun one of them held. "How about it?"

"What do ya think, Erme? He ain't one of the men we seen at the station."

"No, I didn't see any colored among 'em either, Coby. All right, put your hands down. But I'm warning you, we'll be watching you." Erme lowered his shotgun as Shepherd lowered his arms.

"That's better. I want to see the kind of trash that's been killing and robbing pilgrims on this road for the last several months." Shepherd pointed over to where the outlaws were lying.

"Go ahead, Coby. Watch out for him. I'm going back to the women and kids. They're scared out of their minds." Erme turned to leave, disappearing into the night.

Coby walked along with Shepherd.

"I'm Shepherd, Deputy Marshal for the Oregon Territory." Shepherd headed back for the outlaws. "I've been following you all since you left Angelle's." He held out his hand.

"John Coby, Ohio. My partner is Erme Neil. We grew up together. Got married together. Come west together." Coby gave a solid handshake. "You a for-real marshal?"

"Here's my badge." Shepherd opened his vest. "I've sworn and signed on the dotted line. Been shot at and everything. Saved your butt, didn't I?" He struck a match down his trousers and the flare revealed the bodies of the dead outlaws. "Here's the sorry lot. Ain't much to them." Shepherd examined their clothing, before shaking out the match. "Their horses are around here someplace. No identification, just a few dollars in coins."

"You going to bury them?" John cleared his throat. "I hadn't said it, Marshal, but me and Erme is thankful. You showing up was a surprise, is all."

"No, Coby, I ain't going to bury them. That gang should be back looking for them soon. They would think it strange if you did, make them suspicious. You can take their guns and ammunition if you want. The gang would expect that, same with the horses."

"I'll take the guns. Not interested in the horses. Got enough to feed, with our own and the mules."

"I'll keep the horses, then. I can use them. Go back to the wagons. I'll catch up when I finish here. You won't be hard to find." Shepherd rolled the body back into the dust where he found him.

Shepherd spent the night with the young families. "My compliments to the ladies, I ain't et home canned stew, beans, and biscuits with real butter and apple butter in a while of remembrances. A welcome treat to what I had been eating."

"Keep moving due west until you find the river.

Names Hill is a bit south of there, follow the trail. You should be there with another six days of constant moving. I don't think you'll have any more trouble from Lonnie's men."

In the morning, they said their good-byes. "One last word of advice, Tom Dearborn is the manager of the Sutler's store at Ft. Hall, see him for anything you may need. Make a report to the commandant of the fort about what is going on out here. Tell him I am going to find their hideout and try to bring them in. I hope to have this cleared up in a few weeks. Look up the Todds, young couple about your ages, wintering at the fort. I helped them at Names Hill a few weeks ago. You should all travel together. The Applegate Trail is being used more often than the northern route. Easier travel once the snow breaks."

He watched until their jiggling white canvas tops disappeared into the waste of cactus and tumbleweeds. "God bless you folks. I hope you make it. The west needs more like you."

CHAPTER 11

With the outlaws' horses in hand, Shepherd wasn't worried about finding the gang's hideout. He simply let them go. Riding behind, out of sight at a safe distance, he followed.

"Pretty clever of them." Russel and Browney's horses headed northeast and disappeared around a low outcropping about three miles from the main trail. You couldn't see the outcropping from a distance as the ground looked flat in all directions. Gullies ran here and there from flash flooding, carving out a small valley.

With his field glasses, he could see where the outlaws were forted up in a cabin with a porch across the front. A barn stood behind the tank of water next to a windmill. He tied Dusty in a copse of brush and continued ahead on foot.

"Well, I'll be." Shepherd paused, looking at the machine pumping water into the round tank. "I didn't think I'd see one of those. We had them back home, but I've never seen one out west." He was looking at a tower with a fan on it that spun in the wind, pumping water to the surface. "Must have tapped into ground water. If I'm not mistaken, we're not too far from the Big Sandy. Maybe there's an underground river, until it resurfaces, miles from here."

He settled behind a rock where he could hear and see what went on in the hideout.

Browney and Russel's horses walked up to the tank and began drinking.

A hombre coming out of the barn stopped and ran over to examine them, then he ran back to the shack, calling through the door. "Hey, Russel's and Browney's horses are back. No sign of either of 'em."

"Nothing of Browney? Russel? I knew they bought it in the raid. Somebody bushwhacked them for sure."

Lonnie walked out of the shack and stood looking at the horses. "Came here on their own, did they?" He examined them. "'Course this is the only water and they knowed it. Just the same, makes a fella wonder if someone didn't follow. Bitterman, mount up and go look around. See if any other tracks followed the horses here and go look see if you can find their bodies."

A wave of anxiety washed up Shepherd's back. If Bitterman just checked the horses' tracks coming in, he was fine, because he had stayed well off of their flank about a quarter mile. It depended how thorough the rider, Bitterman, was.

I need to talk to Angelle tonight. There's too many to take on all at once. What will I do with them when I get them? Lyle never told me that. He said to wipe them out. I could keep them prisoner in the shack and send someone to Ft. Hall for some help. Yeah, I gotta talk to Angelle, maybe he knows which members of the gang work at the store and when. Maybe, I can catch them in shifts. Those pieces of puzzle were jumbling up in his head, spinning faster and faster.

Shepherd watched Bitterman saddle up and decided it would be healthier for him if he was back at his own camp, as he didn't want to be caught out in the open. But he waited to be sure Bitterman was down the trail before he rode out. As he was about to go, a young man, tall with a shank of thick dark hair, came out of the house with a couple of buckets. He filled them in the cistern and went back into the house.

"Haven't seen him before, wonder how he fits into all of this." Shepherd slipped away, feeling better that he had found where the gang holed up. He rode several miles around the gang's hideout, out of sight, so Bitterman would not cut his trail, and then he rode for his camp near the Big Sandy. "Hope this throws off that Bitterman. He appears pretty salty to me."

Cold winds were blowing in from the north, chilling him. Once he made the river, he followed it northeast to his camp. Checking his back trail, he saw no dust and was satisfied no one had cut his trail.

He fed and watered his stock before building a small fire in his stone stove, setting the coffeepot to boil while he gathered brush and limbs to block the persistent north wind from blowing into his shelter.

Satisfied, he rolled a cigarette as he tried to get the puzzle pieces floating in his head to form a picture of what was happening. He still hadn't figured out the connection between Angelle and the gang. They must have something on him. The big man did not strike Shepherd as a man that is cowed easily. That night at dusk, he went back to Angelle's store.

Angelle carried his bucket out to the corral. "Marshal, yo here?" he whispered as he dumped feed into the trough. "Whoa, Martha, no need to knock Angelle off his feet. I give yo some."

"I'm here, Angelle. Found the gang's hideout. They've got water out there and are well hidden."

"Yo find da hideout? How yo do that? What yo know? Did they attack the wagons?"

"Yes, but we stopped 'em. Surprised them during their attack. Two were killed. What do they have on you? You don't seem like the kind to be bossed around by somebody like Lonnie."

"Ya know Lonnie's name? Er, goo, good." He cleared his throat before he spoke again. "I tell ya what they got, Marshal. They got my boy out dare. Dat's what dae got on me. My boy. I wonder about Russel, when he no show up to guard da bridge."

"I saw your boy, about fifteen, sixteen, tall, dark hair?"

"Yeah, dat's him. Lonnie makes me behave so's they can rob de peoples an I can't do nothin' about it."

"I'll watch out for your boy. What's his name?"

"Name is John Paul. He's a good boy. A bit confused lately. I got's ta go. They watch for me. Yo need som'thin'?"

"Some blankets if you got them. It's getting cold. I'll be back tomorrow."

"G'night, Marshal. You kill 'em all ifs ya can. They is mean killers. I bring some food and blankets tomorrow. Ya be careful, hear." Shepherd watched him go back into the store.

"What is it that nags me about him?" Shepherd still hadn't fit all the pieces into place in the puzzle. Angelle remained an odd piece that just didn't fit anywhere.

Shepherd fetched Angelle's burro to gather wood for the night. He scrounged around the river bank, best he could, with as little noise as possible for enough wood to last him. The cold was becoming another enemy to fight, omnipresent and unrelenting, especially at night. Wind blew continually out here. There was nothing to block or divert it. It was coming from the north, bringing cold gusts that chilled to the bone. The wood would help through the night, and the stone stove would radiate heat into the tiny shelter and keep him warm. He had gathered a thick layer of brush to block the wind coming in on the north side of his dugout.

He liked the little burro and would scratch his ears and

talk to him. The little animal seemed to understand what Shepherd was saying to him.

The burro carried a lot of weight for its size, which was a good thing for Shepherd. He needed the water and the wood the little animal could carry, so he spoiled him, wanting the burro to feel comfortable being part of the camp.

Shepherd roped off one third of the shelter where he could feed his animals but give them room. Their added body heat helped keep the place warm as well. Shepherd prepared a supper of pemmican and desiccated vegetables as a soup and a rock-baked bannock. A hot meal was welcome. If he could get a couple more blankets from Angelle, he would be warmer when the weather turned colder, but for now he was fine.

Something was bothering him. Something didn't fit in the puzzle pieces floating in his head. What was it? On one hand, everything seemed to be coming together. On the other hand, something tugged at his mind that didn't fit. What was it? He went to sleep mulling it over. Somehow, he felt vulnerable, but he couldn't figure out how. His sleep was troubled that night, going from one dead end into another, trying to make those pieces fit.

He woke to a surprise in the morning. The horses were not in the cave. They had pushed through the brush in the back. Dusty and the packhorse were nearby. They came eagerly to his call. The little burro was nowhere to be seen. "Damn, I was just starting to like that little critter. Maybe he made his way back home to Angelle's, or he found a group of wild burros to join up with."

By midmorning, Shepherd was back in a hidden position watching the movement of the outlaws as they came and went from their hideout. Bitterman saddled up and rode to the south.

John Paul and Lonnie went off to the side of the shack and did some practice shooting at cans and wooden targets.

Lonnie was pretty good with his handgun, and John Paul was good with his rifle. Shepherd watched mystified. These men acted too comfortable with each other.

Why is John Paul shooting with Lonnie, like they were friends? Angelle did say the kid was mixed up. What's really going on? Shepherd rolled over on his back to figure this through. Something caught his eye. It was a small seashell. "What is that doing here?" Shepherd was puzzled by the shell, so out of place in this desert. A shadow crossed over his face and a familiar figure loomed up from the scrubby mesquite and sagebrush.

"Tol' Lonnie, I thought someone was spying on us." Bitterman smashed his pistol into the back of Shepherd's head and everything went black.

Chapter 12

"Wake him up. He's been out long enough," Lonnie demanded.

A bucket of water broke through the fog surrounding Shepherd's sleep, startling him back to consciousness.

"Who are you? What are you doing here?" Lonnie peppered questions to Shepherd's face without waiting for an answer. "Were you the gun that bushwacked us? You killed Russel and Browney?"

Shepherd sat tied to a chair, water dripping down his face. He stared at Lonnie for a while then glanced about the room. "Heard you fellas had a sweet deal here. Thought I'd look things over, before I came to see if you needed any more hands. Russel and Browney? Is that who they were? Found two bodies back by the cutoff trail. T'weren't nothing to track all of your horses back to here. Looked to me like you may have needed replacements for those two poor fellas back there."

Lonnie looked at him with thoughtful eyes, tapping his fingers on the tabletop. Leaping to his feet, he groaned with impatience and threw the table away from him. His eyes brightened in wild dilation as he slapped Shepherd's face back and forth with both hands then began hitting him full in the mouth with practiced punches.

Painful flashes exploded in Shepherd's brain, hard enough to knock him back in the chair, before crashing to the floor. The little man could hit hard.

Lonnie put his boot on Shepherd's neck, adding his full weight. "I don't believe you. Damn you. Tell me who you are and we'll go easy on you when we kill you. If you don't talk." Lonnie stopped for a moment in thought. "I've learned a lot from the Indians," he whispered at first, until his voice was lifted in anger and rage. "I can make you scream for days as I burn you up a little at a time starting with your feet and working up your legs. A hell of a way to die!"

He kicked Shepherd's head with the heel of his boot. "Who are you?" Lonnie's face was white as chalk. His voice broke when he spoke as he tried to contain himself.

Shepherd had blood dripping from his lips, hot and sticky. Sweat blinded his eyes as Lonnie bent over studying him, a weird smile on his face. "Get him up. I'm going to enjoy making you talk."

"Like I said, Lonnie, I'm looking for work and I don't care where the money comes from." Shepherd croaked the words from bloated lips and a thick tongue, after two men set the chair back on its feet. Light flashed in his head on and off as he struggled to keep consciousness.

Lonnie hit him on the other side of his head. "You know my name? Tell me your name." He hit him again. "Search him." He pointed to an older Indian standing off to the side. "Crooked Knife, find out who he is." The Indian started searching his coat and clothes.

"Well lookey here, Lonnie. Our new em-plo-ee here has got a badge." Crooked Knife flashed Shepherd's badge before handing it to Lonnie.

Through swollen eyes and lips, Shepherd saw a husky Indian dressed with a military blue jacket and a leather beaded band around his head, hand Lonnie his badge.

"United States Deputy Marshal. Are you the law? Out here? So you did kill my boys and messed up our play." Lonnie walked around the table and poured himself a cup of coffee. Sitting down, he perused Shepherd with an appraising eye. "You must be good or they would have sent someone else. They sent one against ten? Damn, you must be good. What's your name?"

"Shepherd McKinzey is my name." He sat up straighter in his chair. His mind was still foggy. "More men are on their way here right now. I left word back at Ft. Hall when I come through there, where I would be."

"Hey, Senor Lonnie, I think I heard of this Shepherd." Je'sus stepped forward, eyes wide with remembrance.

"Shut it, Jesus. He's a nobody." Lonnie studied the badge in his hand.

"Name matches the badge. How could you leave word where you would be, when you didn't know where you would be? You're lying. Don't blame you, I'd lie if I was in your place right now. Question is, what am I going to do with you?"

Crooked Knife leaned over and whispered something in Lonnie's ear. The conversation lasted several minutes with Lonnie's face going from doubt to delight.

"Crooked Knife has an idea. Deputy McKinzey, you ever hear of John Colter?"

Shepherd paused in thought before answering, fighting for more time to let his head clear. He spoke slowly, "Colter was a mountain man. First white man to ever see parts of Montana, Colorado, and The Great Salt Lake Valley. He was a hunter for the Lewis and Clark expedition."

"You are a smart man, Deputy. Ever hear of Colter's Run?"

Shepherd looked at Crooked Knife then over to Lonnie. "I've heard of it. Everybody has."

"See. I tol' ya he was smart."

"Crooked Knife thinks we should reenact Colter's Run. Can you run, Shepherd?"

"Nothing to brag on," he mumbled. Shepherd looked at Crooked Knife through puffy eyes. The brave stood about five feet, six inches tall, barrel-chested and flat-footed. Pretty typical for an Indian. His age was probably, forty to forty-five. Age was difficult to tell with most Indians. He could be thirty-five just as easily. None of the other men in the room looked like they could run, except John Paul.

Shepherd was in his prime. He guessed his age, about twenty-five. He had never learned his real birth date. The rugged life he had lived since running away from the men who killed his folks had left him muscled, sharp of mind, and in the best shape of his life. He stood six two in his stocking feet and in his younger days had run with the best of them.

Lonnie would never guess John McKinzey (the man who adopted him) had taught him to ride and to fight and could hold his own against anyone. His mind was no longer a painful blur. A plan began a spark in his mind. He would find a way out of this mess and when he came back, revenge would be a cold mistress.

"That's not a very bright idea, Lonnie. When they find me, they'll trace my death back to you. You weren't hard to find. Those men coming will find you too. There's no one else out here but you and your gang."

"I didn't say we were going to do it, Deputy. Colter was chased by Indians: Blackfeet. Crooked Knife is from the Blackfoot tribe. His weapon of choice is the knife and bow and arrow. He has also taught John Paul here, the art of knife and bow. John Paul is a crack shot with handgun or rifle, and he is deadly with a knife in either hand. I've seen him split an apple swinging on a string from fifty paces with a bow. When they find you, it will look like Indians killed you."

"John Paul!" The name shocked Shepherd. Did

Angelle know his son had thrown in with these cutthroats?

"Lonnie, what sport would it be out there? A man's feet would be cut to ribbons in a few yards of cactus and sharp rocks." Shepherd let his voice waver a little. He knew a bully would be sucked in to the sound of fear in his voice. Smiling inside of himself, he thought Jonny would like his trickster coyote pleading. "You can't put a man out there. It's going to be freezing tonight." Shepherd knew it was going to be cold. He'd trade cold for being alive. He just needed a head start.

"Cut him free. Stand up, Deputy McKinzey." Lonnie motioned for everyone to go outside. Shepherd started to get up after his bonds had been cut. He leaned heavily on his chair, favoring his right leg. "Go on, get moving, I said." Lonnie slapped Shepherd's back.

Shepherd stiffly stood, leaning on his chair for support. "I think I busted an ankle when you knocked me over. I, I can't walk, let alone run. Don't do this. It's murder."

"Outside with you. Strip him." Eager hands pulled and lifted Shepherd outside, then tearing at his clothes until they knocked him down rolling him on the ground pulling off his clothes, laughing at his nakedness. Lonnie' eyes were bright again as he laughed at Shepherd's situation. "The Blackfeet had Colter run naked as a jaybird. We must do the same. Get your bow, Crooked Knife. We must even the odds for our marshal. Stand back, everyone. The fun is just beginning. Form two lines. He must run a gauntlet, jus' like ol' Jim Colter."

"Do you think they'll write about you, Shepherd? My guess is you'll be dry bones by spring. No one will ever hear of you. Here are the rules. Crooked Knife will shoot an arrow down the arroyo here. Once you walk to it, the race is on. I'll hold them back 'til you get there. But first, you must run the gauntlet. There are seven of us. Colter had a full tribe. Crooked Knife wants first crack, since Jesse was a friend of his. He starts hunting when you gets to the arrow. After one minute more, I send John Paul. The winner gets to kill you Marshal, anyway he wants and for as long as he wants.

After I get tired of waiting, say twenty minutes, if I don't hear from either one of them, I send the rest, either riding, running, or flying, however they want to. They all go." Lonnie walked around his men, raising his hands into the air, shouting, "Kill Shepherd! Kill Shepherd." Grinning like a leering weasel, Lonnie led the chant. "Kill Shepherd. Kill Shepherd."

Shepherd didn't know how Colter must have felt to hear hundreds of warriors screaming for his blood, but just hearing it from the seven men surrounding him, made his blood run cold. He was shivering as it was. The wind was from the north. The arroyo was about 100 yards long before it turned to the left beyond a pile of boulders. They would be out of sight once they made that point. Shepherd tried to find his direction. Wind out of the north. His camp lay to the south. He would be running west when they started.

"Are you cold, Deputy? That wind is all mighty brisk, don' you think? Once I catch up to you, black man, we is going to have some fun, jus you and me." Crooked Knife reached out with a stick with an eagle claw on the end and cut him across the chest. Jibes from the other men filled Shepherd's ears. He hung his head, but down deep within him, he knew he was going to win in the end. He would be back somehow, someway.

"Shoot the arrow, Crooked Knife." The Indian lifted his bow and drew back, shooting into the air. Everyone's eyes were glued to the arrow shaft as it rose up in a beautiful arc and came down in a descending arc, once it had reached its zenith. It fell out of sight in the sagebrush, about eighty yards straight ahead.

"Get going, Shepherd." The men brandished sticks and rocks, ready to strike him as he passed.

"I, I cain't. I'm freezing."

"Get going or I'll kill you right here." Lonnie fired off a round close to Shepherd's feet which started him down the alley of leering men screaming for his blood. He used his arms to ward off the blows as best he could. Crooked Knife slashed with a knife. Shepherd veered like a drunken man to avoid being stabbed.

Je'sus jabbed him in the side with a sharp stick, starting another stream of blood. Ducking a fist-sized rock aimed at his head, he tripped and received a kick to his stomach, but he scrambled to his feet, turning and ducking as best he could. With a last effort of will and a building hate, he fell forward in the dust at the end, bruised, battered, and bleeding but alive and burning with a deep anger that was going to sustain him through the rest of the run.

Crooked Knife and John Paul jerked him to his feet. Shepherd studied the boy as he was up close to him for the first time. His eyes held the same crazy light as Lonnie's. Shepherd involuntarily felt gooseflesh creep up his back. This John Paul was a killer!

He limped purposely, fighting for time, trying to catch his breath and focus his eyes.

"Begin." Lonnie shot his pistol into the air.

Slowly, Shepherd started down the arroyo, leaving hoots and catcalls behind him, careful of thorns and sharp rocks, using this time to look around him for anything he could use. He kept his eye on where he knew the arrow fell and gathered himself for a fast start. There were no sticks. No branches big enough to use as a weapon. Sharp, pointed Spanish Sword cactus pierced his flesh; sharp rocks and stickers pierced his feet.

He could use a rock, but he didn't pick up anything, it would slow him down. Avoiding the taller thorn brush and cactus that threatened to rip his vulnerable flesh, his feet kept being snagged by low-lying thorn and prickly bushes. By the time he reached the arroyo, he was dribbling blood and limping for real. He tripped over a tangled vine, banging his shins on a knee-high boulder. The arrow stood planted in the ground on the other side. He grabbed it, and tore off with an unexpected burst of speed to the surprised onlookers.

"Damn, he was faking the whole time. Crooked Knife, go." Lonnie cursed at being tricked.

The lithe Indian leaped like an antelope. His heavy, muscled body was rippled and smooth as he raced along the ground, yelling his war cries, closing the gap as his prey rounded the rocks and disappeared from sight. He was fast for short distances. The Indian in him would make him go when his body felt the searing pain of muscle fatigue and burning lungs.

The point of the arrow is chipped, thought Shepherd as he ran for his life. His fingers explored the stone arrowhead and the broken end of the shaft, feeling a broken point without looking at the arrow. His eyes searched for a way. An escape. A weapon. Anything that he could use. The best he could find was in his hand already.

He turned to look behind him as Crooked Knife made the turn for him, running at full speed. Shepherd ran to his right and knelt down behind a boulder on one knee. The arrow was in his right hand. He had to do this the first time, because young John Paul was right behind them. The Indian came around the boulder at full run. Shepherd thrust the broken shaft into his midsection, up to where his hand stopped and blood gushed down his arm.

Four Finger's eyes bulged in surprise as he gasped, burbling blood in his mouth. Shepherd pulled him down to the ground and struck his chin with his left fist, knocking him out. He tried to pull the arrow free, but it broke off in his bloody hand.

"Running men, two. Blackfeet, nothing. I wonder how John Colter felt after he killed his first Blackfoot, before he hid out in that beaver lodge?" Shepherd grunted. "Some folks just don't learn." He threw the piece of arrow away and pulled off the dying Indian's boots, quickly pulling them over his bloody feet and grabbed the blue jacket with one hand. Shepherd unbuckled the knife belt, pulled it free with the other. He didn't have time to put them on.

John Paul was beating around the first turn as Shepherd smashed Crooked Knife in the throat with a sharp rock, finishing him, then he turned and ran for his life. Wrapping the jacket around the knife belt, he slung it over his shoulder as he ran.

Shepherd bolted through the rough countryside with Crooked Knife's big knife clenched in his other hand in a white-knuckled death grip. Still naked, thorns and sharp rocks tore at him as he raced past, but he paid no heed to pain and fatigue. Death was flying after him in the form of young John Paul. His eyes searched the ground before him for something, anything that could give him an advantage. He glanced back to see Angelle's boy closing the gap.

John Paul was fast. He flew like a jackrabbit with a cocky grin on his face. He was so confident he would win that he didn't see Crooked Knife's body, until he tripped over him, falling head long. Scrambling to his feet, he uttered an oath, drew an arrow, canted, and released.

Shepherd just ran with everything he had, tripping and stumbling over loose rocks. One stumble saved his life. The arrow swooshed down just inches in front of him, nipping his right shoulder as it fell. Shepherd cut to his left, running between some boulders, then he ran right. He felt his shoulder. He was bleeding as it had ripped the skin, but he would not stop. Stopping meant dying. Shepherd wasn't cold any longer, but he was getting winded. His feet hurt, but the coldness made them numb to the pain.

They raced for another mile, John Paul slowly gaining ground. When blood started dripping from his nose, Shepherd knew he had to make a stand before he was completely exhausted. Shepherd held the knife in his hand.

He had to catch John Paul off guard. The younger man was gaining. Shepherd knew he was in for a fight for his life. Cutting to his right, back to the south, he hid behind a pile of boulders mounded up about twelve feet high. Gasping for breath, he blew the blood from his nose and mouth then peered around the rock, looking for John Paul. Stooping low, he picked up a round rock about the size of a large apple, expecting the hunter to come around the corner like Crooked Knife had. There was no movement. He looked again. No one.

"I'm over here, Marshal." John Paul was behind him with an arrow in his bow.

Shepherd was trapped between John Paul and the rocks.

"I think I'm going to scalp you. Not many scalps like yours. The Indians will pay a fine price for it. First, I'm going to use you for target practice. Left knee first." John Paul loosed his arrow.

Shepherd leaped to his right. The arrow shattered against the rock.

"Oh, Marshal, you are fast. Let's see you duck an arrow in your gut." John Paul already had another arrow nocked and ready. He raised his bow.

"EEE-aaw! EE-aaww!" John Paul startled and glanced to this right. Burro came through the brush and right up to Shepherd. The arrow shot down between Burro's feet.

Shepherd dove forward, his knife at the ready. John Paul was pulling his belt knife when Shepherd sliced through his right side.

John Paul clutched at the wound, spinning and slashing for Shepherd with his left hand, leaving a bloody trace on his leg, but the move caused him to lose balance. He grasped at Shepherd as he fell.

Shepherd smashed down with the rock in his left hand, hitting John Paul just below the back of his head, breaking the vertebrae. John Paul rolled on the ground, his body quivering in death convulsions, then he relaxed and lay still, his eyes staring at the dust and cactus.

The little burro came over and nuzzled Shepherd's hand, making him jump in surprise. "Where did you come from, little guy?" Shepherd knelt down beside the little burro, soaking in his warmth.

Realization that he was not finished jerked him back to reality. *Rest and die* flashed through his brain. He stripped off John Paul's clothes and put them on. He kept Crooked Knife's jacket. He kept both knives and took the bow and arrows. Wrapping a neckerchief around his leg, he staunched the bleeding. Already he could hear the yips and cries of the other men in the distance coming for him.

"Let's see if we can fool them." Shepherd mounted Burro, his legs dangling at his sides and made off away from the arroyo at a ninety-degree angle to the south. He left no human tracks that way. It was getting late. The sun had about an hour before it set. They needed a place to hide for the night, but first, Shepherd wanted to get away from there as fast as he could. He urged Burro onward, a few light kicks and off they trotted. Shepherd gave the animal his head as he didn't know where to go. Maybe the burro would.

Something in his mind flashed at him. John Paul bore a resemblance to Lonnie. He had noticed it as they took his clothes. From a distance, it wasn't noticeable, but up close, it had caught his attention and lingered in his mind. Pieces of his puzzle were becoming more and more at odds with themselves. He needed to look at this from another angle.

"Let's go, little brother." Shepherd urged the burro on. His weight didn't seem to faze the animal at all and they took off in a direction known only to his trusty steed.

"Whar is he?" Je'sus rode around the body of John Paul, looking for tracks. "Ah cain't believe he killed them both." All the men rode up, struggling with their mounts to hold still, while their eyes roamed over the terrain looking for their prey. "Senor Lonnie is going to be very unhappy. The boss is not goin' to be happy neider. I don't envy this marshal when we catch up to him. John Paul was the boss's favorite, now he is dead."

The more they looked, the more the area got chewed up by horses and the men searching the rocks and hillsides. There were no tracks leaving the area. Shepherd had vanished into thin air. Only wild burro tracks crossed the area. No one paid any attention to them. Reluctantly, the men gathered the bodies and took them back to the hideout.

Lonnie was beside himself in fury. "No one is that good. He was god-damned naked, for god's sake. He had no weapons and yet he kills off my best men. He killed my brother, the best man I knew with a gun or a knife! How does that happen? No tracks? Did he fly out of there? Are you all idiots," he screamed. "There is some kind of sign, we just aren't seeing it. We can't see anything now that it is dark without messing up any tracks that are left. Get some sleep. Tomorrow, we find that son of a bitch or I'll kill all of you, trying."

Chapter 13

S unset was glimmering over the horizon, casting orange and yellow lights, backgrounding the low shadows forming on the cooling desert. Shepherd's burro made directly for a fallen slab of rock that had slid off of the rim rock, eons ago. It had come to rest with a narrow declivity between it and the rock face. Time had allowed sagebrush and mesquite to grow and tumbleweeds and brush to collect around the area covering the entrance. Local animals visited here for its shelter and a way out of the wind. Shepherd couldn't believe there was an opening until Burro stuck his head through the brush. He just walked up to it and went through like he knew it was home.

It was dry inside the slab wall. Shepherd dared not build a fire for heat as the light could be seen for miles. He guessed the gang had given up for the night as he had left no tracks. They would be back in the morning, scouring the countryside for the killer of their companions. Burro had walked over five miles through rough terrain that would leave little trace. He must find a way to retrieve Dusty and his gear.

He needed a gun, rifle, and a thick steak with onions and fried potatoes cooked in a cast-iron skillet over a hot fire, some buttered biscuits, and a slab of cherry pie. He enjoyed that image in his mind for a brief time. Food was continually on his mind. He made up his mind to be hungry and live with it. He had not eaten all day. His next meal was just as far off as his last. The immediate need was to survive the night. First, he inspected his wounds. Except for the stab wound to his leg, the rest were superficial bleeding. He powdered some sage leaves between his fingers and bound that over the wound on his leg with his bandana. The cut on his shoulder stung but had stopped bleeding. He ground more sage between his fingers and packed it into the wound. The tiny pricks and thorn tears in his skin, he did the same. It would have to do. He had clothes at least. John Paul was closer to his size than Crooked Knife. Pulling up some of the brush within his nook, he stomped on it to smash it flat to serve as a bed to get him off of the ground. A lot of petting and ear stroking coaxed the burro to lie down next to him, giving him warmth on one side. Pulling the jacket over his shoulder helped keep some body heat. A lot better than he expected, when he watched the arrow arch through the sky that afternoon and felt he may never see another sunrise. He slept like the dead.

He was cold when he woke but no frostbite. Jumping up and down, swinging his arms and hands, he had to work his joints with his hands to stimulate his stiff limbs. His left leg was painful to stand on but no longer bleeding. Burro and jacket had kept him warm enough to get some sleep into the chilly morning.

Frost covered everything when he peeked outside. He saw white shimmering desert in the early morning dawn. He crept back inside, as he didn't want to leave tracks or a disturbance that would draw attention. The gang would be out circling, looking for spoor, of that he was certain.

Inventorying his resources, he had two knives, a bow, five arrows, and some flint arrowheads found at the bottom of John Paul's quiver. Tucking one of the arrowheads in his knife belt, assured Shepherd he could make a fire. He felt confident a fire would not be seen in the daylight. There would be smoke, but it would burn clean and the smell of the sage, that was everywhere. Gathering some brush, he managed a tiny fire using the arrowheads and the steel of a knife to make a spark. The dry tinder eagerly grew into a little fire that felt wonderful to his hands, giving off faint smoke.

As his body warmed up, confidence and intent began to creep back into his spirit. Shepherd contemplated what he was going to do, while he appreciated the warming flames. He had to consider several scenarios as he did not know how they would come at him. If nothing happened with the gang, he would have to take the fight to them. He knew he had to end this one way or another. He preferred his way.

Once the hoarfrost had evaporated on the vegetation with the rising sun, he put out his fire. Shepherd scouted around his shelter. He had to find some type of defensive strategy. He estimated the rock slab to be about twenty feet high. The slab leaned against the rest of the rim rock from which it broke off, leaving an overlap pointing to the sky, close to ten feet tall.

Off toward the north, he could hear shots every now and then as the gang tried to roust out any hidden Shepherds they suspected of lurking in the brush. If they were any kind of trackers at all, they would begin to circle soon.

Bitterman was the one Shepherd was leery of. He was wily as a coyote and vicious as a snake that had been stepped on. Shepherd knew that if they found him, he would be killed on sight.

He climbed the shelf rock and used the jutting rock shelf as a watch tower. In this place, he surveyed the desert for the men he knew would come. To his north, riders scattered over the land, studying every overturned stone. He could hear shots, shooting into anything they thought

Shepherd could hide in. He watched and waited all morning.

A speck appeared over the tops of baked brush and bramble to the north. Sun waves shimmered over the desert as the black figure bobbed up and down getting closer and closer. From the moment Shepherd saw the black speck, he knew. Bitterman. Bitterman had figured it out. The black specter rode in a straight line. He no longer was hunting. Shepherd realized that Bitterman knew where he was or that he was at the end of the trail he was following. Shepherd lay flat out of sight. He had prepared for this.

Bitterman pulled up after he spotted the slab of rock, figuring this was where the tracks of the little burro led.

"Come out, Marshal. Don't make me come get you. Come out. It won't be pretty if I have to come inside to get you." Bitterman pulled his pistol and shot in the air. He rode closer and shot at the bottom of the slab, sending a shower of shards in all directions. "I said come out!" He rode closer and shot into the cave itself.

An eruption of brush and brambles exploded as Burro burst out. Bitterman's horse reared and danced on his hind legs. Bitterman was an excellent horseman, but the burro surprised him and he didn't have a secure seat. He fell on his back swearing and cussing his horse, searching for his gun in the rocks.

"Hell-o, Bitterman. Meet my friend Burro. I'm Shepherd. I am up here." Shepherd stood with arrow nocked and drawn.

Cursing, the outlaw lurched for his gun. As he cocked his pistol, Shepherd shot him in the chest, pinning him to the ground with a quivering arrow. Bitterman stared up at him, struggling to bring his pistol up. His gun dropped from his hand as his body slumped to the ground and his spirit fled.

Shepherd scrambled down the face of the stone, checking to make sure the wily outlaw was finished. He couldn't believe his luck. "I'm going to keep that little Burro. I like him."

Now he had what he needed. He took Bitterman's clothes, his guns, and horse. Searching through the saddlebags, he found some pemmican and cold biscuit. He gnawed on the hard pemmican like it was a bone. Water from the canteen was next, then he washed his biscuit down and smacked his lips. "Yes, sir, a steak is just what I need." He smiled at his joke.

Shepherd mounted Bitterman's horse, wearing his vest and coat and broad-brimmed hat over his face. He loaded all weapons. Two pistols and extra cylinders from the saddlebags were in his belt or pockets of the vest. Dusk was about an hour away.

He rode to the shack from the west, riding loosely. The sun at his back made him look like a shadow as he approached the hideout. Burro was tied by his halter and brought up the rear. "He's saved me twice, I'm keeping my lucky burro with me."

"Rider comin' in. Looks like Bitterman's horse. What's that behind them?" Several men stood up on the porch looking into the sun as Bitterman rode up, trailing a burro behind him. Lonnie came out to see what was going on.

"Did you get him, Bitterman? You found a burro? Hey, did you get that marshal?" Lonnie called toward Shepherd.

Shepherd rode closer. "Yeah, Lonnie, I got me." Shepherd raised his head and opened fire, wounding Lonnie in his left arm. Both of Shepherd's hands were filled with guns blasting away, knocking men off of the porch like bottles off a fence rail.

Lonnie retreated back into the shack, firing into the air. Shepherd was busy returning fire with a shooter close to the shack's door and couldn't follow. A good shot creased the shooter's temple and he fell like a sack of cabbages.

All was quiet. Shepherd got off of the horse, guns ready, eyes darting everywhere for any movement at all. He pushed the door open and waited. Nothing. He threw his hat through the door. No response.

The shack was empty. Shepherd could see a window had been broken out. Lonnie was gone. Going to the window, he could see the dust still hanging in the air from where the bandits had made their getaway. He turned to go back on the porch for anyone he had missed.

Reloading his pistol as he came back out, he saw Je'sus sitting on the top step of the porch, looking at the bodies. He was bloody and dying. "Damn, Shepherd," he gasped with his last breath, staring, "you didn't give us a chance. I knew I had heard a'you. They said, you is a bad man to cross." Jesus rolled over and bounced down the steps. Dead on delivery.

"Just like you gave me." Shepherd walked around checking the bodies, making a body count. "Just like you would've given me."

"I count eight men down so far, including Russel and Brownie. Lonnie was the ninth man. Who is the tenth? Did he ride off with Lonnie?"

Shepherd had to keep that in mind. Ten men in the gang was the number Lyle had given him. "Who was the tenth man?" Puzzle pieces were starting to fall into place, but some still didn't fit and it troubled Shepherd to vexation. "What am I missing?"

The sun had set by the time Shepherd watered and gave some green hay to Burro and Rocky. Inside the shack was a cold pan of stew, a tin of cornbread, and a pot of cold coffee on the table. He helped himself while he gathered the outlaws' guns and outfits. He would have Angelle send someone to bury the dead.

He kicked over a tin box on the floor. Examining it,

there were some bills still in the bottom. "Lonnie's cash box." In his haste, Lonnie must have made off with what he could grab and crashed through the window to escape. He would turn it in to Lyle when he got back.

"Must be a hundred dollars here." Shepherd rolled the cash and put it in his shirt pocket. "Wonder how much Lonnie had made off with?"

Shepherd couldn't leave the gang's horses to starve, so he decided to take them to Angelle's. In the morning, he would pack up the guns and ammunition he found. No one would leave this much ammunition and guns for curious Indians to find. They would look like a pack train moving through the desert with Burro trotting along.

He had thought to burn the place down but decided to leave it. The windmill was the only water source in the country. It seemed a shame to destroy it. Maybe some pilgrim would settle there. Burro helped drag the bodies into the barn where Shepherd covered them with hay. It seemed the decent thing to do. He would have to spend the night in this house of death. It could be worse. He closed his eyes under the first roof over his head in weeks.

CHAPTER 14

Twelve horses followed Shepherd back to Angelle's, by the Cutoff trail. He doubted he could handle that many horses and a burro going through the tiny cut he had cleared to cross the river, so he threw caution to the winds and rode the main trail. The clattering of all of the horses on the bridge brought Angelle out to the porch.

He stood leaning on a post, slack-jawed as Shepherd pulled up with twelve horses.

"Damn, Marshal. You got dem all?"

The thick Cajun accent dripped off his lips as the big man examined the horses, with his eyes darting over to look at Shepherd every now and then as if he couldn't believe it. "You got dem all?"

"Lonnie and one other escaped. I wounded Lonnie. Didn't make out who the other man was. They broke out a window. Grabbed the cash in the cash box and hotfooted it out of there. Got what they left, in my pocket. I haven't seen them since. I don't suppose I could get some breakfast, before I see to the horses? I am looking forward to a steak if you have one and a half dozen eggs or so. Some beans or potatoes or both. A good cup of strong black coffee would set real good."

"Shure, Shure, come on in." Angelle played with the

buttons on his shirt as he looked back at the horses as if he was looking for something, then he changed his mind and waved Shepherd inside. "Come in here, Marshal. I fix you up something good. I eat it myself. I do got a steak and lots of eggs. Beans is done in few minutes and I get some taters frying. I fill you up. Coffee is over on the stove, hep yourself, I just cooked it. I was expecting Lonnie and the boys, ya know. I wonder what happens, when no one showed up yesterday to guard the bridge. You broke up da gang? By yoself? Dat is somthin." Angelle's dark eyes searched Shepherd's face, before turning back to the stove.

"Two are still out there." Shepherd sat back, blowing on the coffee in his cup. He looked at Angelle. He didn't seem to be as happy as Shepherd expected him to be, now that the bad guys were out of his store. He liked the big man, but something was picking at his mind about Angelle. He should be happier that the gang was broke up. Instead, he seemed nervous. Was he afraid Lonnie would come back for him? Did he know John Paul had joined up with the gang?

"Here, yo steak and eggs and beans. Taters ready in a minute. Yo want a bread? I got some prickly pear jam. Goo' stuff on bread. Make it myself. There you are."

"You can send someone to see to the burying? I don't want to leave them in the barn for too long, even in this cooler weather." Shepherd gestured to Angelle with his fork after eating some beans.

"You left dem in the barn? Dat is good. Coyotes don't mess with them there. I know some Indians that will do ta job for a couple dollars a piece. Here's your taters."

Shepherd tossed six dollars on the table. "There's two apiece for the Indians and two for the breakfast. That's good. Food looks mighty inviting. I've been feeling my stomach gnawing on my backbone." Shepherd ate with a smile of satisfaction on his face as he savored the first bite. He ate slowly, enjoying each morsel. Angelle poured a cup of coffee and sat down by the stove, watching him eat.

Shepherd felt pleasant and warm here. The first hot breakfast, or meal for that matter, he could remember in a long time. Angelle had a clock on the wall that ticked off the time. The fire in the stove was burning low, emitting small pops and cracks from wood burning down into glowing embers. It was quiet except for Shepherd's knife and fork clattering together as he ate his food. A quiet which grew heavy.

Shepherd looked up at the heads of wolves, buffalo, and catamounts mounted on the walls as he enjoyed his meal. Those dead eyes seemed to be staring at him. Tick, tick, tick, pop, pop, crackle, crackle, Shepherd was strangely affected by all of the eyes staring at him. It was eerily quiet except for the tick, pop, tick, crackle, pop, tick, and fall of ashes crumbling into the fire pan. It was unnerving. He laughed at himself and glanced over to Angelle to tell him the odd sensations he was feeling.

Angelle sat, staring at Shepherd with black, cold, bottomless eyes as dead as the sightless animals on the walls as he rocked slowly back and forth. His coffee cup was still in his hands clutched between his knees.

"You ain't mentioned my John Paul. Did he rode off with Lonnie? I seen his horse out dere. Tinking maybe it was he, dat rode off with Lonnie on another horse? Or is dare something you ain't told ol' Angelle yet."

The giant stood up, glowering at Shepherd. He slammed his coffee cup on the table. His body so huge, it blocked the warmth from the stove. He put both hands on the table and leaned forward to get close to Shepherd's face.

"Is dare something you ain't tol me yet?"

A cold shadow blocked the light in the room. Shepherd looked up at Angelle. The same Angelle he had seen the day they met. An angry Angelle. A behemoth of dark fury searching Shepherd's face for answers he already knew. A dark fury that would know if Shepherd lied.

"I thought John Paul was being held as a hostage, Angelle. He tried to kill me. They put me through a Colter's run in the desert, naked with no weapon. He was one of the men Lonnie sent to run me down and gut me. Did you know John Paul and Lonnie were friends? He did not act like he was a captive."

"Dae were brothers, by differt mamas. Lonnie was da oldest. John Paul always looked up ta Lonnie. Lonnie was supposed ta teach him." Angelle's voice minced his words in a hushed whisper, hands opened and closed as he stared at Shepherd.

"Teach him? You. You are the tenth man. You are the boss!" The pieces of the puzzle clicked into place at last. Shepherd looked over at Angelle as realization snapped the puzzle pieces into the final clear picture. His face relaxed with satisfaction, then a growing dread started at the back of his legs, traveling all the way up his spine.

"Yo right. I am the boss. John Paul was my favorite an yo kill' him. You kill them all, ceptin' Lonnie. How yo do that? I tol them about you and dae laughed it off. A black marshal clear out dere! How could it be?

"So, I play you, Marshal, like I is you friend, so's I know you plan. Except you got no plan. No plan you tell Da'vid about. And now they all is dead. My John Paul is dead. Pretty soon, I gonna make you dead, too!"

For a huge man, Angelle was surprisingly fast. He charged around the table, animal moans erupting from deep in his chest as he grabbed for Shepherd's neck.

Breakfast forgotten, Shepherd dove under the table, scrambling for the other side. He ducked when Angelle lifted the table and threw it across at him, scraping his shoulders and neck as it flew over his head. He was trapped between the table and an angry bull. No time to think, Shepherd vaulted the table and headed for the door.

Angelle could move. He caught Shepherd from behind

as he opened the door. Snatching him back in a bear hug, he used his treelike arms lifting him over his head like a sack of meal, and threw him through the door.

He landed outside amid splinters and broken wood, dazed and breathless. Struggling to his knees, he realized he was in a fight to the death. He brushed off the splinters, trying to steady himself against the wall of the building.

"Hey, Marshal. I's comin for you." Angelle burst from the store, pinning Shepherd with a death grip. One hand held him around his neck and the other searched his pockets. "Gimme that money, yo say you got. It's mine." He ripped the pockets from his vest until he found the bills.

"I gonna kill you now. How you kill John Paul?" He picked Shepherd up by the shoulders and shook him. "How you kill hem?"

"A, a, a, rock. I hit him with a rock."

"Noo? A rock? You kill my boy with a rock?" Angelle threw Shepherd to the floor of the porch, pressing him down with one arm, glaring. "You lie! No one could kill John Paul with a damn rock." He smashed Shepherd in the head with a meaty fist and began shaking him again. "Tell me the truth. I'll shake your eyes out, I will. I fix you now, like you kill my John Paul." He threw another fist into Shepherd's face. "You stay dare now." He lurched himself up then went down the steps of the porch.

Raising himself to one elbow, Shepherd watched the backsides of Angelle merge into the shade of an old bent pine. He shook his head, struggling to make his eyes focus. Feeling more in control, he drew his gun as Angelle bent over to pick up a large river rock about the size of his head. "That's enough, Angelle, don't make me use this. I took it to the others. I won't hesitate to shoot you."

"I don't care. You kill my boy. I kill you."

The big man lifted the large rock over his head with both hands and moved toward him with obvious intent.

Shepherd shot Angelle's left hand, causing the boulder

to fall on the madman's head, knocking him out cold. The Cajun collapsed in a lump of hairy, angry flesh.

A sigh of relief washed over him. Realizing it was over, Shepherd staggered to the trough, shooing the rooster away. He dipped his bandana in the water to wipe his face and neck. Tired beyond remembrance, he leaned back against the cool trough in the shade for a few minutes, staring at Angelle's still form, so at peace.

After a few minutes, he staggered over to where Angelle lay piled up in the dust and nudged him with a toe. "What am I going to do with you? I can't drag your big ass by myself."

Burro to the rescue again. Shepherd wrapped a loop around Angelle's shoulders, and Burro dragged him over to the nearest tree.

"I can't lock you up. There's no place strong enough to hold you. I'm going to tie you so you'll have some movement but can't stand up." Shepherd struggled to bind him to the tree, cursing the man mountain the entire time.

Being unconscious, Angelle was cooperative as much as his flaccid slabs of arms and legs would allow Shepherd to move them.

He inspected Angelle's head. There was a pretty good gash across the top, blood dripped over both ears. The left hand was missing two fingers. Shepherd dressed them with the juice of some of the cactus growing by and powdered some sagebrush into the wounds. He wrapped them with some bandages from the store. With a grin, he wrapped the gigantic head in swaths of bandages completely covering Angelle's eyes and head.

Picking up Angelle's fingers in the middle of the yard, he threw them to the chickens.

"Now I don't have to look at you." He left Angelle bound to a tree with wraps around his torso and legs with knots tied in the back of the tree. His prisoner could not reach around to untie himself, so he left the arms free.

Placing a water bucket in the shade, so the giant could have water, Shepherd went in to explore the store to see if he could discover anything else.

He reasoned that since Angelle was the real boss, it only made sense to look around the real headquarters.

Shepherd's concern was to search the store for evidence. He had to figure a way to get the enormous Angelle back to stand trial without having to bind him from head to foot like a trussed fowl, to prevent him from getting away and to keep his prisoner from killing him at any moment.

Inside the store, he set the table back on its legs, retrieved his steak from the floor. Eyeing it with dismay, he stared at a skillet on the stove. Stoking the fire to flames, he wiped off what was left of the steak and placed it back in the pan. He fussed with it, poking the fire until his breakfast began to sizzle.

"Maybe, I'll get to finish my meal." Poking into Angelle's desk, he didn't find much. No one had kept a record of the robberies or how many they had waylaid over the last year. Some nice furniture was piled up in one of the rooms. There were trunks of women's clothes and shoes, men's hats and worn boots. Many rifles and shotguns were stored alongside barrels of flour and rice, coffee and beans.

"They kept a storehouse of stolen goods and sold it off to pilgrims as they came by and stole it again to resell to the next victim. According to Erme and Coby, the gang's prices were extravagant. The robbers made money coming and going. They robbed the emigrants with high prices in case they didn't get to rob them on the trail. Since most of the traffic was one way, there was no one to report the robberies and murders farther up the trail. The only way they came to be reported were from relatives missing their families when they did not arrive at Ft. Hall, who then complained to the superintendent of the post."

Shepherd flipped his steak. Smelling the aroma of

sizzling meat, he rejoiced with appreciation. His appetite had returned. Salting the steak with gusto, he contemplated if he wanted some eggs, as his were scattered on the floor.

"Hey! Hep! I've gone blind. Am I dead? My head is killin' me. Wha you do ta me?'

Shepherd walked outside, the steak impaled on his fork. He took bites from it as it pleased him. He leaned against what was left of the doorframe and watched Angelle struggling with his bonds.

"Don't take those bandages off your face. You've lost two fingers to your left hand."

Angelle stiffened. "Who's dere?"

"That rock must have hit you harder than I thought, who do you think it is, big man? It's Marshal McKinzey."

"I gonna kill you."

"Yeah, maybe you will, we all must die someday, but it will not be today of all days. Today is not my day to die. I think Jonny, my brother, read that to me once. Some English King."

Angelle started to pull at his bandages.

"If you pull off those bandages, your head and your hand will start bleeding again and you will not get that chance to kill me as you desire, because I'm not getting close enough to dress them again. I covered your face, because I am damn tired of looking at your ugly mug."

Angelle started struggling again.

"Okay, be stubborn. If you don't sit still, I will bounce that rock off of your thick, fat head once and for all, just like I did John Paul. Do you hear me? There's a bucket next to your right hand for water. I'll bring you a blanket and some food later, but you stay where you are or this will be your last day on this earth. The more I find out about you, the less I am willing to put up with you. Burro can drag a dead body out into the desert just as easy as a live one."

"Wha happen to my fingers?" Angelle was clutching

one hand with the other, trying to count his fingers.

"I threw them to the chickens, you big heap. They looked hungry, scrawny as they are. You have any wagons in the barn?"

"Go stuff yourself, Marshal."

"All right, I'll go look for myself. Leave those bandages alone." Shepherd walked to the barn, chewing on his steak every few feet. He would look back at Angelle sitting back against his tree, holding his left hand in his right, looking like a body that had only been partially shrouded.

He pushed open the sliding barn doors. This was a part of the barn he hadn't been in yet as the feed and hay were stored in another room. There were several wagons, loaded with belongings of departed pilgrims. Shaking his head with disgust, Shepherd wondered if he should give Angelle the luxury of a jail cell. It would not give him a second of guilt if he simply put a bullet in the behemoth's brain and be done with him.

"This will do." He appraised an empty, canvass-less, prairie schooner which stood in the corner by itself. Shepherd climbed into the bed, deciding what he wanted to do. Using a blacksmith's hammer, he drove large metal staples into the thick sides of the wagon strong enough to chain Angelle to. Pulling a tarp over the first few hoops, he then filled the bottom of the wagon with straw.

"Accommodations of the house, Mr. Angelle. Ring for service when you want your bed turned down." He threw an old horse blanket in the back and was finished. That was as comfortable as he was going to make his prisoner. There was room in the wagon for hay, grain, and water for the animals to make the crossing.

Shepherd stretched his back to relieve some pressure and as he did, something caught his eye on one of the crossbeams supporting the roof. A tin box, just like the one he had seen at the gang's shack was pushed into a corner of the barn's rafters.

Shepherd moved the hay ladder to where he wanted to climb. Peeking up from his perch on the ladder, he saw there were two boxes. He retrieved both. One was filled with cash, the other with gold coins. The gang was rich and they never got the chance to spend it. Shepherd bowed his head at the thought of how many people had lost their lives for this money and now it would go to the state. A futile lesson in greed.

Shepherd crossed back to the tree Angelle was tied to. "I found your cash boxes." He shook them so the gold coins clinked. "My written report will be enough to get you hung, Angelle. I hope I am there to see it. They will have to order a new, thicker rope for you."

When he was done, he turned the horses into the corral for feed and water but left the gate open so they could come as they pleased. He didn't want them starving. He took the ones he needed to the barn for grain and rest. Maybe some pilgrims would take the others. Supplies, they needed to make the desert crossing, would come from the store. He would be ready to leave by morning.

He used a pitchfork to goad Angelle into the wagon, yelling threats to impale him with it if he tried anything. Satisfied his prisoner was securely chained to the wagon, he gathered supplies and stowed them in the wagon. After he was finished, Shepherd ate an enormous uninterrupted breakfast. Angelle got a cup of coffee and a biscuit with ham.

As he crossed the bridge the next morning, the last thing Shepherd saw as he looked back at the store the next morning, was the sunlight playing on the golden-winged angel on top of the building. The early sun made the angel glisten in golden light. A beacon for all new pilgrims arriving that would be a sign for hope rather than death. He left a note on the door that read, "All Who Enter Here Help Yourself. United States Deputy Marshal, Shepherd

McKinzey, Oregon Territory."

CHAPTER 15

Marshal Lyle entered Delmonico's intending to meet with Delmonico's owner. Out of the corner of his eye, he spotted Quinn in the back of the room sitting with a young woman. Sudden inspiration overtook his good manners. "Quinn, I've got a job for you if you'll take it," he yelled over the din of the crowd, waved, and quickly moved toward them.

Quinn saw Marshal Lyle when their eyes locked in the dining room of Delmonico's in Salem. He looked away quickly, turning to the attractive lady beside him. She was beautiful and smart, and full of witty banter, all tempting assets to his liking, and he was planning on spending the evening with her. Lyle was a friend, but he always had bad timing.

Lyle moved through the busy restaurant avoiding waiters and fat men's cigars as he wove through the crowd. He had just observed a high-stakes poker game in a third-floor suite above the restaurant, as he had been hired to ensure everything about the game was honest. That's why he was meeting Jim Jolly, the owner.

Delmonico's had the best steak in town, and Lyle was looking for a low-keyed dinner with his friend, Jolly, but he was in a jam. He hadn't heard from Shepherd, and the man to get him out of that jam, sat in the back with his female companion. He knew it was now or never, when he caught Quinn's eye at the back of the dining room.

"I am lucky to see you here." He doffed his hat to Quinn's companion, whose smile dropped at the sight of him. "I've got a job for you, if you'll take it." His eyes surveyed Quinn then the lady beside him.

"Lyle, good to see you." Quinn was dressed in his best clothes and shined black leather boots. "Just arrived in town a few days ago. Need to check in with Shepherd and the ranch. Brought in another train of green horns and pilgrims. 'Cept they ain't as green as they once was. They'll do. Planned on lookin' in on you too, Marshal."

"That's just it, Quinn. Sent Shepherd on a mission and I haven't heard anything from him." He took a chair from a neighboring table and sat next to Quinn. "Usually, I get updates from my deputies. He's late. You're just the man to go after him."

Quinn stood and proffered his hand toward his companion. "Marshal, this is Miss Lilly Trout. Judge Trout's daughter."

"Pleased ta meet ya, ma'am. I remember you as a child with pigtails and bare feet."

"We're pretty occupied here, Marshal. Is this something I can talk about in the morning?"

Lyle shook his attention off of the young lady and looked dumbfoundedly at Quinn. "Tomorrow?" His eyes cleared. "Of course. Make it seven. I'll have coffee ready. Miss Trout, a pleasure seeing you again." He turned and left the room.

Quinn's face drained a little. "Seven?" He watched Lyle's back as he walked out-of-sight into the next room. He whispered under his breath, "I guess, I'll see you at seven." He gazed at his lady. "Seven, tomorrow morning." He grimaced.

Lyle folded the paper in his hands as someone pounded on the door to his office at 7:30 a.m. "Come on in. You're late."

A pained expression wore on Quinn's face as he came through the door and sat in the chair next to Lyle's desk. "You sure throw a thorn in a man's evening, Lyle. We argued all night if I was going to do what you asked. I had promised her a picnic and some horse riding. Hell, she even wanted me to show her how to shoot a pistol."

"Sorry, Quinn. It's about Shepherd. Jonny's out getting married to that Shoshone girl he fell so hard for and he's not around. I felt lucky to find you in town. We can talk, but I need a yes or no." Arguing his case, he stepped forward to explain the urgency to Quinn, when the door opened and Colin and Phineas Stuart burst in.

"Oh, excuse me, gentlemen. Good morning." Colin touched the brim of his hat. "This fellow is me uncle and we need your help, Marshal. I also have some papers for you to sign about some cases going before the judge."

The elder Stuart stepped forward brandishing his cape. "I can introduce myself, Nephew. I am Phineas Stuart, I'm being hounded by British bounty hunters and they are illegally pursuing me on American soil. I've broken no law in this country of USA. I ask for your protection."

"Mr. Stuart, I am finishing some business, I will be with you as soon as I can." Lyle gestured to the wooden chairs against the wall then turned his attention back to Quinn.

"Quinn, ya gotta help me out. Shepherd may be in trouble and I've got no one else."

"I'm here, ain't I? Of course I'll go. Never was a question of it. I coulda wished for better timing, however."

Phineas Stuart stopped in his tracks, startled by what he heard, and turned back to the marshal. "Did you mention a Shepherd? Perhaps a Marshal Shepherd McKinzey?"

Lyle and Quinn turned to the Scot. "He's my deputy. Do you know him?"

"Indeed, I do, friend. We shared camp not more than a fortnight ago. A good fellow. Taught him aboot good whisky. He has an appreciative mind. We got along. Is he in a wee bit of trouble?" Phineas used his thumb and forefinger to indicate a small measure.

Lyle raised his arms as if in submission. "I think he may be in a heap of trouble. I haven't received any dispatches from the fort. I don't know where he is. I'm asking Quinn to go find him and help, any way he can. Shep is a tough bird. I wouldn't want a tussle with him, but I haven't heard from him and he is overdue. We need to find him."

"Ah…Marshal, thank you. Thank you." Stuart came forward with an engaging smile on his face.

"What?"

"I'll gladly travel with this fellow. Shepherd told me about both of you and how proud he was to be your friend."

Lyle stepped back and rubbed his chin. "I know you now. You're the Scottish rogue Shepherd spoke about. A British agent did stop in the other day making inquiries about a thief they were chasing. They were looking for the likes of you." He stepped forward and took up Phineas' hand. "I'm proud to meet you. Not fond of how the British push everyone around. I've heard your story from young Colin, here." Turning toward Quinn, he looked to him and said, "What do you say to this, as a traveling partner?"

Quinn rubbed his jaw as he walked around the elder Scott, seemingly in deep thought, then he sprung forward in a feint.

Stuart's stick went up to Quinn's throat, and his hand filled with a short full-bladed sword from beneath his cloak in a flash.

Quinn smiled to Lyle. "I think he will do." He offered

his hand. "My name is Quinn—Mr. Stuart, I would be honored to have you accompanying me."

"Come join us, Mr. Stuart." Lyle waved their new companion over to them.

"Quinn, do you know anything of the Greenwood cutoff or Sublette's cutoff as well?"

"I do as a matter of fact, Lyle." He poured himself a cup then sat on the desk looking at Lyle. "I heard at Ft. Hall there was some chicanery going on out there. Mostly rumors, nothing nobody knew for sure. Is that where you sent Shepherd?"

"Yes, it is. I sent him to the Greenwood cutoff. They're starting to call it the Sublette Cutoff for some stupid reason. Greenwood was the first to suggest it."

"When do you want me to leave?" He looked over at his new companion. "Er. When do you us to leave?"

"As soon as you're ready. Get a packhorse from Bandy at the blacksmith's and I'll authorize Artie at the store to bill the territory for your supplies. When you're ready, I'll deputize you again. Send word back along the trail with wagons and travelers you meet on your progress and tell them to report to me when they get into town so I can keep track of you. It's harder and harder to keep track of my men. One of these days, someone will figure out a way to send messages quicker than horseback, but I don't know how."

"Let me finish my business, gentlemen, and I'll get out of your way. Just sign here and here, Lyle." Colin smoothed some papers out flat and pointed where he needed Lyle's name. He looked over at Quinn with a question in his eye. "Which way you headed?"

"Reckon, I'll head south first, on the old Siskiyou trail then head east to Ft. Hall. Too much snow in the northern passes right now, so the southern way is where we're going."

"Well good luck to you. Shepherd is a good man." He

waited for Lyle to sign his papers.

"By the way, I'm going to need extra food and blankets, for Stuart as well. It's going to be cold," Quinn interrupted.

"I want you to have what you need, Quinn. The Territory can afford a few blankets. Mr. Stuart, do you have any questions? I'm not deputizing you as I'm not certain which country you belong to." He pushed the signed papers over to the attorney. "Colin, I will see you in court tomorrow."

"Yes, you will, Lyle. Uncle Phineas, watch out for yourself on the trail. Hope Shepherd is all right out there alone. I'm sure he can grind his own corn, but it's good to know you're going to join up with him. See you all later." Colin went outside.

"I'm not getting anything done here either. Guess we'll get going," Quinn said to Lyle, who was studying reports in front of him. He held the door for Colin as he exited out the door.

Phineas moved to follow. "I know the Siskiyou. Need to pack me own gear. I'll meet you down the trail aboot nightfall. Keep an ear out for me. Just a few personal tings I always carry for me self." Phineas nodded to Lyle and exited the office.

"Whoa, Quinn. First things first, this is the second time I've sworn you in as deputy. I don't suppose you want to make it permanent?" Lyle dug a badge out of a drawer and tossed it on the desk.

"If it's just the same to you, Lyle. My daddy used ta say, 'Never be the servant to any man or job long enough to wear out your boots.' I lived my life on that one principle an I'll just be comfortable in these boots, but not a forever job. Which is why I like being a scout. I'm a man on my own when the job is done."

"All right, but the offer is always there. Mind your hair. You all come back safe and I hope to see Shepherd with you, next time we meet."

CHAPTER 16

Q uinn made his preparations wondering what in the name of sense he was doing! He didn't know where Shepherd was in the Sublette Cutoff wilderness, much less what to expect from Colin's uncle. "Guess I'll start asking questions at the fort," he said to himself as he mounted his ride. Clucking to his horse to get going, he pulled the reins with his left hand and wrapped the leads around his saddle horn with the right.

Three sets of eyes watched him leave town then turn toward the split off for the Siskiyou Trail, south of town. It was the main highway for all travelers, trappers, miners, and native tribes for several hundred years. At its height of popularity, it stretched from Canada to Mexico.

Slowly they walked their horses, keeping a good distance from the sight of Quinn's back. "Since we lost that Scott, we follow Quinn. From what Peeping Tommy told me, they are going to meet up somewheres south of town on the old trail." James Slaven reined his mount forward picking up the pace.

"I thought we had old Phineas. Tommy could always

ferret out a secret for the right price. He's always been on the money. How Colin got him out of the courthouse without us seeing him is a mystery. Let's catch up to this fool and beat it out of him. I want to sleep in a warm bed tonight, not some mucked-up bedroll. Whatta ya say, James? Let's bushwhack this fella and get back to town."

"I hear you, Martin. We need to be far enough out of town, not to alert anyone. Be patient. I think you will have your bed tonight. Now quiet. Follow me and back me when I have a want of ya. The Crown is paying a pretty penny for Stuart. Let's be sure we have our chicken in a sack this time."

An hour on the trail, and Quinn was humming a song that came to mind. "Camptown Races," a song he had loved all his life. "Do dah, Do dah," when he stopped abruptly, looked behind him, then started riding again.

Prickles rose up his back. He was positive he had heard horses coming behind them earlier. He had just heard those hoofbeats again. *Someone was following him.* He had been too long a scout on many wagon trains, not to know that someone was following his trail.

He quickened his horse to a lope then rode about half a mile and pulled up in a brushy maple thicket after rounding and descending a sharp hill that crossed a cold, flowing stream. He backed into the thicket out of sight, pulled up his double 00 shotgun as he loosened the loop over his hammer on his gun belt. He freed the revolver from its holster and dropped it easily back into place making sure it was clear. He waited.

The three men who rode past him wore English greatcoats, vests, and woolen trousers. *British agents!*

As they rode by, he kicked his heels and his horse sprung onto the trail.

"Gentlemen."

They turned toward him.

Quinn lowered the shotgun and moved his jacket back off of his hip, clearing his revolver. He kept the reins in his left hand and he laid the right hand to the right of the pommel, close to his side. "I like to know who's keeping company with me."

Slaven rode forward. "I'm James Slaven. We're looking for a theivin' Scottish rogue by the name of Stuart. We have reason to believe you may be meeting with him."

"And you are?" Quinn smiled. He didn't like this one little bit. His horse sidestepped, but he sat his saddle well, keeping the double barrels aimed waist-high. "Whoa, Bob." He reined the horse over so they still faced the trio of riders.

"Let's say we have some unfinished business with that Stuart fellow." Slaven moved to Quinn's left, a smirk on his face. The other riders spread out in a semicircle, facing Quinn.

"You're the British agents Lyle spoke of. Well, as you can see, he ain't here. He was in the marshal's office yesterday, the last I seen him."

"Our agent says, you two are to meet up south of here."

"Look, I don't care what you think you heard. Go back to Vancouver and get out of our country. You have no jurisdiction here." Quinn's horse spooked to the right. He grabbed the saddle horn with one hand and leaned with the horse, staying with him. "Damn it, knot head, whoa, Bob."

Slaven looked to the agent on his left and the man jumped his horse into Quinn, swiping at his head with his revolver.

Quinn blocked the blow then spurred his horse into the other rider, throwing both off-balance, dumping the other rider to the ground. Quinn creased his scalp with the barrel of his shotgun, and the man known as Martin dropped onto the trail and rolled into the stream.

Both Slaven and the other man reached to draw their waist guns.

Quinn still held the shotgun. "Look, before we blow each other to hell, I'm not meeting your damn Scot. This is what I know and I'll tell you as a sworn deputy of the Oregon territory. I have no allegiance to the man. He told us he was going back over the border for some warehouses that have been recently filled by the Trading Company. Now let's drop our weapons and move on. I've got a friend to find. That's what I'm after. The Scot is your business."

"I think you're lying." Slaven and his agent thumbed the hammers on their guns, kicking their mounts forward.

Quinn blasted them with 00 buckshot, knocking both out of their saddles. His next shot scared off their horses. He rode over to check the Brit's condition. Slaven was bleeding from his left shoulder. The other man had two 00 buckshot holes in his forehead. There wasn't much of the back of his head left.

"You called the play. I answered. Go back to Britain. I'll report this to the territory." Quinn reined his horse around and galloped down the trail, bringing the errant horses back.

He saw Slaven shake some sense into the man in the stream and watched them mount their horses as he left. "That ought to throw them off Phineas' back for a while."

Toward the afternoon, he pulled up under a Ponderosa Pine to get out of the sun. Quinn pulled out the makings and rolled a cigarette. As he took his first puff, he looked up into the yellow eyes of a full-grown catamount lying on a limb about ten feet from his face. Quinn froze.

The cat snarled, and his scent filled Bob's nose. The horse jumped straight up, throwing Quinn off in a pile, then landed on all four feet bucking as hard as he could. Quinn skidded across nearby rocks and tree roots, bruising muscle and limb. The packhorse shied away as the bucking horse ran into it then ran with cat scent wrinkling his nose.

Screaming intimidation, the male cat leaped over Quinn's head, running like a house on fire, vanishing down the trail following the spooked horses.

He lay still until he was sure the cat had gone. "Damn, hell and tarnation!" Quinn fumed. Pushing himself to his feet, he shook out his joints and limbs, sore and stiff, but nothing was broken. There was no sense in trying to run down the idiot horses. He realized he was left afoot. Vexed at the entire situation, he walked over to a fallen log and made another attempt at rolling a cigarette, trying to keep his hands from shaking the tobacco out of the paper. After several attempts, he gave up and flung it to the ground.

Clip-clops sounded on the hard trail, and his packhorse came drifting back with his head hanging low. "Whew, you're a sight for my eyes. At least I won't starve." He stroked the horse's neck and took the bridle and tied him to a stout tree nearby. "I hope that cat leaves my Bob alone. I'll sure miss him, even if he is a knot head."

A snarl sounded through the trees, right behind them, causing Quinn to jump. He held the bridle of the packhorse, to keep him from bolting again. Swinging around, he drew his pistol, seeing the yellow eyes gleaming through the thick underbrush. "Come on, damn you. I'll send you to hell." He fired two shots, clipping the base of the spruce tree over the head of the leering cat.

The lion slipped away silently into the forest, leaving Quinn eyeing every leaf that moved until he was sure the devil had fled.

"Whew, I am as nervous as a house cat and a rocking chair," he laughed nervously and sat back onto the log. "Those big cats can be sneaky, coming in from behind you. I've seen them rip a man's throat out and haul him onto a tree branch. Hell, I'm even talking to myself." He tried again with the cigarette, successfully rolling a suitable one, then took a long satisfying drag on it, calming his insides.

He knew he had to keep his guard up. That cat could come from anywhere in the thick forest. A snarl from farther up the trail caused Quinn to jump again, soon followed by a horse's screams.

Quinn stepped out on the trail, seeing Bob running full tilt toward him, stirrups flapping up and down with each pounding hoof. Waving his arms, he stopped the frightened beast, calming him with soothing strokes and a soft voice. A raw claw mark showed on his left flank and his sides heaved. "Well, ol' Bob, I look pretty good to you, don't I, boy? Think twice before you run away from your buddy, Quinn, next time, won't you?" He dug through his saddlebag, finding a tin of ointment that he gently applied to the wounds. He then hauled off the saddle, dropping it next to the fallen log. "Guess we make camp here tonight, boys. I don't want to be on the trail in the dark with a hungry cat in the vicinity. 'Sides, he's already got a taste of horse flesh. He might come back for more."

Later, after he made camp, Quinn rolled a bannock around a clean stick and stuck one end in the ground and positioned the other end over the fire to bake, while the rest of his food cooked over the coals. His senses were on full alert if the cat had come snarling around the camp before nightfall.

One of the horses snorted and looked behind him. Quinn stepped away from the fire so he could see better, listening to the sounds of the night which had become mysteriously quiet. Leaves shuffled a little. His packhorse blew a soft snort.

Quinn waited. Holding his knife in one hand, the other on the Paterson in his belt. Something rustled behind him. Spinning, he drew his gun.

"Supper smells good. It be a burning a mite." Phineas

stood over the fire poking the potatoes roasting in the fire with a stick.

"Tarnation! You scared the living bejesus out of me, Phineas! How did you get behind me?"

"I have me ways for stayin' alive, my boy. For a share of your supper, I'll swap a wee draft of whisky." Phineas rubbed his hands together as he surveyed the camp then pulled his bedroll from his horse next to him and dropped it close to the fire against a log on the ground. Kneeling, he rummaged around in his haversack extracting a bottle of clear amber liquid.

"Got a plate? I need to turn this bannock so's it don't burn like the rest of the supper. Not a great hand at cooking now, is you?" Quinn moved the stick so his bread would cook evenly.

Phineas raked some potato and onion onto his plate and cut into the broiling meat, adding it alongside the rest of the food, then licked his fingers after. "Sure are jumpy tonight, Quinn. What's got you het up? I'm beholdin' to you, that you don't mind some company on our mission to find Shepherd. I can drag me own weight and toot me own horn. I'll not be a bother." He looked at his friend with a question in his eyes.

"Had a tangle with a big cat today. Scared off my horses and drew blood on one of them. He's been skulking around here all day, darting into and out of the bushes. I've been nervous as hell. I almost shot you just now." He knelt next to the fire, poking at his hot food, trying not to burn his fingers as he reached for a tin plate. "I am glad to see you. I can use the company. I've had the jitters all day."

Quinn stabbed the rest of the food with his fork and onto his plate. "I'm used to it burnt a little." He studied Phineas' horse and pack animal. "You brought supplies too. You ain't no green bean. I'll not be nurse-maiding ya on this trip. We're going after desperate men from what Lyle told me. You sure you want to get mixed up in all of that?"

The Scot broke off a piece of the hot bannock and folded it over the potato and onion then popped it into his mouth. He cut a piece of the meat, pillowed that in a puff of bread, and followed that down his throat. "Haven't et all day, trying to catch up to you. I might as well tell you the whole of it. The damn British are looking for the likes of me. I need to get away for a while, till they simmer down a might. I hate the British and I'm not a favorite countryman of theirs. I can be of help to you if you take me. You won't have ta worry about me. I'll watch out for ye an I know a few tricks when dae wind blows up your back."

"I had a run in with them British boys this morning. They were following me looking for you. Had to shoot one of them, they was pushing way too hard. Told that Slaven fella a big lie. That you was intending to rob His Majesty's warehouses. That should keep them off our tail for a while." Quinn ate in silence. He liked Phineas' demeanor. "Ya look pretty salty to me. I suppose you brought a gun or two?"

"Aye. I've got me pistols and a rifle and I carry a scatter gun for close quarters. Too bad you didn't kill the whole lot, laddie. That Slaven has been extra keen to get his hands on me. Glad to hear he's headed back north." He sat down and moved a short sword out of his way. "I've always got me sword close by. Most men aren't familiar with sword play these days. Scares 'em when ma naked blade is exposed." His face turned a warm curious look toward Quinn. "Would ya like a wee dram of whisky?" He held the bottle up for him to admire.

"I do, when I can afford it," Quinn replied, looking at the liquid in the bottle and the beaming expression of Phineas. He knew he was beholding a man in his element. "Especially after that damn cat scare I had today."

"It is a precious thing and should be enjoyed with reverence and joy. The sweet sweat of angels ta be sure. Best to share with a friend, but rightly enjoyed on those nights when you are alone and wishful. Tonight, I make a new friend." Phineas pulled the cork and waved the top of the bottle under his nose. He passed the bottle under Quinn's nose but never gave it to him.

Quinn nodded in appreciation. It simply smelled like good whiskey to him and his mouth watered.

Phineas poured three fingers into a glass that seemed to magically appear from his sack then did the same to his own.

"Na, wait a moment. Swirl it in your hand to warm it a mite and let me shake just a few drops of clear spring water into ye glass. Helps open the whisky. To your health, Quinn, and to the success of our journey. Did I ever till you how the Scots invented navigation?"

Quinn settled on his bedroll, his back against the log. For the first time all day, he felt the tension seep out of his body. He listened to Phineas spewing out story after story of what the Scots had invented, the fire warming his outside and the fiery spirit warming his insides. The happy Scot chortled on. The Scots seemed to have invented everything worth inventing. If they could make as blessed a drink as what he held in his hand. He wouldn't bet against it.

CHAPTER 17

It was a long trip to Ft. Hall. Da'vid Angelle was trouble from the time they left. Shepherd had to chain him tightly in the wagon or else the huge man rocked from side to side threatening to turn the wagon over. He had to put an ankle chain on him so he could do his business in the bushes and then chain him up again. Carrying a pitchfork so it could be seen was enough to encourage his prisoner when he put him back in the wagon. Angelle couldn't be trusted long enough to be fed or for him to sleep without being chained, so he lived in the wagon. Shepherd rested much easier knowing Angelle was securely locked in chains, even though he felt the repugnance of having to do it.

"You're staying locked up in chains since you can't behave. Believe me, I know what it is like and I wouldn't do it. But I know you'll escape or kill me at your first chance, so locked up you're goin' to stay. Take my word for it. I know how to lock you up. I know how it's done. If you're uncomfortable, it's your own fault."

Shepherd hoped Ft. Hall had a cell strong enough to hold Angelle. Taking the big man all the way back to Salem was not something he thought he could handle by himself. Too long with too many distractions. "If I have to chain him in the stable, I'm going to do that. This Territory needs more stations where we can keep the men we bring in. I'll talk to Lyle about it."

"Marshal."

"What, Angelle?"

"I need to stop. I got an ache in my back."

"I'm sure you do. All the people you killed wish they could feel pain in their backs. Shut up and go to sleep."

"I sleep all da time."

"Your problem. We'll be at Ft. Hall by this afternoon. I'll be glad to put you in a nice cold cell. Now be quiet."

Stopping at the noon hour to rest the animals and get a bite to eat, Shepherd was collecting dry sage branches when he spotted a wagon top over a long sloping hill to his east. There was no smoke to indicate a fire at someone's camp. Then he spotted two mules free of their traces, grazing in the brush nearby. Curiosity raised the hairs on the back of his neck.

His breath came quicker as he instinctively stooped, seeking cover. Something was wrong. Sweat wet his hair as tiny droplets formed on his temples and back of his neck. Breezes from the east wafted to him with the answer he knew he would find. Death. He smelled death on the wind.

Circling around behind the wagon, he saw vultures fighting over the remains. A man and a woman had been strapped to a wagon wheel. Their hands stretched over their heads, a rope around their necks. A bullet hole in their head. A pitiful sight.

He shot two vultures and chased the rest away. He had shot in disgust and revulsion. Vultures keep the prairie clean of death's decay, but he couldn't help himself. These people were black. The first he had seen on any trail. He felt like Angelle had just bashed him in his belly. It took several minutes to collect himself.

A pick and shovel were in the back of the wagon. Shepherd started digging, shooting in the air occasionally to keep the birds off until he was done. It took over an hour before he had a shallow grave dug in the cold stony ground. It was the best he could do. Somehow he couldn't help wanting to take his time and do it proper for these two strangers.

Burro again was brought to drag the bodies. Shepherd had to be careful. On his first try, he had pulled the man's feet off with the rope. The bodies were diminishing, even in the cold climate. It made him wonder how long they had been there. The cold weather slowed the decomposition. The state they were in told Shepherd they had been there awhile, maybe a week. Death stench permeated the sleeves of his shirt.

After he laid them to rest in each other's arms, he searched through the wagon hoping to find something to identify them so he could leave a name with the grave. An old family Bible lying beside an overturned trunk caught Shepherd's eye.

Earnest and Pokey Thompson was written on the first page of their Holy Book in a bright-blue ink. There were dates from their family history and an entry when they got married. A brief note written on a linen sheet of paper in bright-blue ink in the same neat hand, revealed the beginning of their journey from St. Louis. It lay folded and placed between the leaves of the book to press.

Softly, he read,

"Ernie and I start our adventure, leaving from St. Louis, with great hope and love of God. We plan on starting a new life in Oregon. By our own hands we will make our fortune. I sew ladies' dresses and make baby clothes. Ernie makes shoes and leather goods for men's fashions and harnesses for farm work. We are joined by our new friend Hannah, who seeks to start a new life as well. God's blessings on us all. Pokey Thompson, 1850."

"Hannah?" Shepherd looked around. There were no more human bodies. A dead mule lay on its side, the vultures scrambling over it, since they couldn't get to the Thompsons. This killing had Lonnie's name written all over it. The fourth mule that was missing must have been taken for the Hannah, Pokey Thompson had mentioned. Everything in the wagon had been rifled through and strewn about. An empty metal box with the clasp beaten off spoke volumes to Shepherd. Lonnie had their money and their friend Hannah. Starting a fire, he heated a thick piece of wire red hot and burnt their names in a board he had pried off the side of the wagon. "Rest in Peace, Pokey and Earnest Thompson 1850"

He went back to fetch the Bible Pokey had written in. His feet kicked at something under the wagon he had not seen before. A large black rag doll lay face down covered by dust.

"Would you look at that?" Shepherd held it up and shook the dirt off. It felt odd in his hand and after turning it over, he found that it was tied up the back underneath the clothes and something was inside the doll. His fingers fumbled at the knots, struggling to untie them without tearing the material. It was an old doll; he could tell from the stains on the faded cloth. The only black dolls he had ever seen were cornhusk dolls, painted black, made by black mamas for their daughters. They were usually hidden away from their white overseers. This doll was about a foot long filled with tufts of cotton wool and made with brown cloth. A face with brown eyes and a smile had been painted on the front. Black yarn was sewn for hair. A gingham apron was made with a yoke around the neck and tied in the back.

The knots gave way. Shepherd paused. He felt he was invading a stranger's private property. Probing with his fingers, he found a linen bag, containing a small hardbound book, which he carefully slid out.

He opened the book to find a photograph of a pretty black woman wearing a hat and a high collar. She had a strong-willed look. He found her attractive. There was also a braid of black hair, a sachet that smelled of patchouli oil, a smell he recognized from his days in the white fight clubs. Black women in these clubs always smelled of patchouli. It was considered very French and provocative. He read the first page of the journal.

My name is Hannah. My mama named me. I have been called other names, but since I have met new friends and am beginning a new life, I want to be called by the name my mother gave me. I don't remember my mother's name, only that I called her mama. I was sold as a young child and never saw her again. I was nine years old. I was raised in a plantation house near New Orleans.

The religion I learned was taught by Catholic nuns, but what I practiced was called Voo Doo, as taught by the women on the plantation. Later, I was schooled by some Urseline nuns and learned some nursing and learned to read and write.

I loved books, often lost in the stories they told. My owner sold me to a man and I have traveled up and down the Mississippi, owned by one man or another for many years. The only things I am good at is playing poker and keeping my current man happy enough that he doesn't beat me often. I am very good at poker. I am a survivor. That was my life.

But that was a long time ago. I met the Thompsons in St. Louis after I ran away from the Steamboat Natchez. The captain was trying to accuse me of killing a man. I knew I had no chance against what he said, so I ran away as fast as I could.

I met Pokey in a market. We became friends and she invited me along with her and her husband Earnest, to travel with them on the trail to Oregon. We will begin a new life. I am frightened of the new and unknown, but more scared of going back to my old life. This is my journal of our travels.

April 1, 1850.

There were more notations, but Shepherd snapped the journal closed. He couldn't bear to continue reading. He would read a little at a time when he was by himself. Right now, he was too emotionally caught up in Hannah's story. He tucked the sachet in his shirt pocket so he could be reminded of her. There was still Angelle to take back to Ft. Hall. His gut told him Lonnie must be behind these killings. His heart debated between duty and wanting to find this mystery woman. An inner war tore at him, but duty won out.

Grim determination knotted his stomach. He returned to his wagon, threw a vicious look at Angelle, and stepped over the side rails. He took off his shirt and rubbed Angelle's nose in the death stench, wrapping it around his head until the big man trembled, retched.

"Get up!" He stood, cracked his whip, and then slapped the reins over the backs of the mules.

"What's got your ass, Marshal? Where ya been so long?" Angelle asked as he threw the shirt over the side of the wagon.

"I found more of Lonnie's work back over that hill. My advice to you right now is to keep your mouth shut. I'm in a killing mood. Just one speck of trouble and I will gut you and stake you out on this prairie for the vultures to finish. I would enjoy it."

Angelle stopped his next words and looked over the hill, the way Shepherd had come. He pulled the blanket over his head and lay down. He didn't speak another word until they came to Ft. Hall, and Shepherd was glad for the peace.

A grim Shepherd pulled into Ft. Hall in the late afternoon. The ground was frozen from the dropping temperatures and his back was sore from the jolting seat over the hard, uneven ground. Snow smelled on the air, mingling with smoke and odors from the fort.

He pulled up in front of the commandant's office. Stiffly, he climbed down and stretched his back and hips and knees as he looked the fort over. Stifling a big yawn, he removed his gloves, flexing his fingers as he disappeared into the door of the office.

He came out a few minutes later with a paper in his hand. Folding it into quarters, he put it into his pocket and went down the steps looking toward the barracks. Three guards appeared from around the corner of the building and waited for Shepherd, at attention.

"Okay, big man. I've got you new accommodations." Shepherd put his gloves on before he unlocked Angelle's chains. "These three guards are to escort you to a new home until we can get a judge to hear your case."

"Ya told me, you was taking me to Salem."

"Yep, I did. Seems the new Territory is better organized than I figured. Judge rides the circuit every four weeks. You'll be hung with a very strong new rope before the new moon. I hope.

"Take him, boys. If he tries to get away, shoot him dead. If he catches hold of any of you, shoot him. Don't take no chances. Don't let him get close. He'll squeeze the life out of you if he gets a chance."

"I'll see you, Marshal, I ain't forgetting John Paul. I still owes ya for him."

"I ain't forgetting all the people you killed either. Murdering bastards like you always seem to blame someone else for the wrongs they did. John Paul deserved no more than what he got. I'm asking around, hoping to pick up some leads on Lonnie. I'd like to see all three of you dead, for the filthy scum you are. Now move along."

CHAPTER 18

O ne of the guards caught his attention by his slackness, as he observed them getting Angelle out of the wagon. "Guards! I tell you again, he is dangerous, shoot him if he tries to escape." Shepherd watched the three uniformed guards move Angelle off toward the stables. He chuckled to himself. The only room big enough and strong enough to hold the giant was where they stabled the stud horses. It had iron rails around the top and they could chain Angelle to the strong posts. They would keep him under guard day and night.

He decided to go to the Suttler's store after he finished feeding and stabling the horses, hoping he could find Tom and catch up on news around the fort. Maybe…someone had seen Lonnie or this woman Hannah. She seemed to occupy his mind.

He drove the wagon over to the post's stable and turned the team over to the young corporal who welcomed him. As he was about to head for Suttler's, he caught sight of the little burro, who had followed all the way from Angelle's place.

Smiling to himself he said, "Hey, Burro, it's warmer in the barn, isn't it?" He led the animal to a small open stable and fed him some corn then forked some straw into the stall so the little guy had a place to lie down.

It dawned on him as he was rubbing the animal's back, here he was putting people in jail or killing them if they were dangerous. Just a few degrees of a different point of view from the slave owners he knew. He paused in thought. *What the hell am I doing? Am I any better than they are? Can he do this just because I am disgusted and repulsed by the people I brought to justice? Is it that plain and simple?*

On the other hand, there were the Thompsons and the mystery of their friend Hannah. He had to admit, their deaths had affected him more than any other death he had seen. What had happened to Hannah? He didn't know and it gnawed at his gut.

He checked with the stable master and transferred the horses to the fort, while his mind played on those questions. Pondering his thoughts as he walked over to the store to talk to Tom, he was startled by a figure standing in front of him.

"Marshal. Shepherd? What a surprise to find you here." A friendly hand appeared before him.

"Ah. Oh, it's you, Todd? Bill Todd. Right. Sorry, I was lost in thought. How are you, Bill? You're settled here at the fort? Your wife, I believe was Frieda, wasn't it?" Shepherd shook the proffered hand with a smile of recognition.

"Oh yes, we are set for the winter. Going to be a cold one tonight from how that wind feels."

"Did you meet Erme and Coby? I recommended they look you up. Thought you all being about the same ages would hit it off."

"We did meet them and we hit it off as you say. We're going to be traveling together once spring breaks. If you don't have plans for supper, I'm sure the rest would like to visit with you and find out how you dealt with the gang. We all owe you a debt of gratitude. Coby shot a big elk a few days ago and we still have some fresh meat. Frieda,

Sissy, and Bethany would love to hear news of the big city of Salem."

"Are Sissy and Bethany, Erme and Coby's wives? I had forgotten their names, since we last met."

"They sure are. Sissy is Coby's wife and Bethany is Erme's. Frieda was sure happy to meet some other women. She's grateful for that. Will you come? We have plenty."

"I'd like that, Bill. I'm bunking in the barracks tonight, but a hot supper with friends sounds too good to pass up."

"Okay, then. See you about six o'clock?"

"I'll be there." He watched the man walk away.

Then it came to him. That's why he was doing the job he was doing. For the Thompsons, for folks like Bill, Erme, and Coby, their wives, and future families. All people seeking a new life needed men like him to do this job. The future of Oregon and all points pilgrims were traveling to, depended on him to make it safe so their families could live in peace. He set people free by locking up or destroying the element that would never change. The evil part that always seemed to be there, underlying the skin of humanity. "Must be a part of all of us too, that evil. Just comes out more in some people."

He wasn't like the slave owners at all. He saw himself more like a deputized vulture, cleaning up the decaying mess so the rest of the forest could grow and flourish and not be overwhelmed by the garbage that always seemed to be a part of any culture.

He wondered about the woman called Hannah, such a pretty name. She hadn't left his mind since he learned about her. Last evening, he had read a few passages from her journal with the Thompsons. Their journeys were so similar. It felt like they had traveled parallel trails.

He dared not linger on how Lonnie would treat her, or his imagination would go crazy. He pulled the small sachet out of his pocket, held it to his face for a brief moment. Gusts blew his hat and he was lucky to grab it before it sailed off. He shivered beneath his mackinaw. Gray skies burdened with snow loomed overhead. Fat fluffy flakes mixed with the wind swirled about his face, hiding the ugly fort in a frozen coat of feathery snow.

As he opened the door, the wind picked up colder, more demanding, blowing snow down his neck.

"Shepherd. It's good to see you again. How ya be? Did you find the men you was looking for?"

He closed the door and welcomed the warmth within. "Tom! Yes, thanks to you and some good luck, I did. I've got the gang's head man locked up in the stable. I hope he stays there." Shrugging out of his coat and wiping the back of his neck, he said, "Tom, I thank you for this mackinaw, it has kept me warm."

"Yea, 100 percent pure wool, nothing better. Comes in assorted colors if you like black and red." He smiled at his joke. "How about a wool scarf? Helps to keep your hat on in a fierce wind."

"Sounds good, I'll take you up on that."

"You stayin' here at the fort? Passes up north in the Blue Mountains are closin' up."

"No, I'm going back, as soon as I get things settled here. Someone I got to find. I'll be back for more supplies when I'm ready to leave."

"Glad you broke up that gang. That's the best news I've had in a while. Are you taking him back with you?"

"No, I'm leaving him here. Circuit judge will show up in a few weeks and a trial will put him away for a long time, hopefully busting rocks in a federal penitentiary. If'n they don't decide to hang him after the judge sees my report."

"I'm relieved that's the end of that. People have enough to deal with, besides their own kind preying on 'em. Anything else I can do fer you?"

"I didn't get everyone. Fella by the name of Lonnie is still alive. Found some of his work on the trail to the fort, burned wagon and two bodies. Took a woman with him, I think. A black gal. I was wondering if you had noticed a short man with a bullying attitude. Dresses kind a fancy, wears a silver belt. Likes to show off. Maybe turned up a week or so ago?"

"Not to recollection."

"Seen any black women about?"

"Haven't seen any black women for sure. Hard to say about the man. Always new faces showing up, short, fat, tall, or lean, all sorts from everywhere in the world."

The door of the store blew open, followed by cold air and wisps of snow whirling in. Shepherd stepped back as two men entered with their heads down, wrapped against the bitterness. One looked up and spoke with a familiar tone.

"Well. Ain't we lucky! Just the man we come lookin' fer."

Shepherd recognized Quinn's voice. Phineas Stuart put his shoulder into the door, slamming it shut against the blowing wind and cold. Both men made their way over to the potbellied stove, taking off their gloves and warming their hands.

"As if I didn't have enough trouble." Shepherd walked over to greet Quinn. "Who's this? Phineas, is that you? How did the two of you meet up? Is something wrong? Somebody die I need to know about? What in tarnation brings the two of you out here in the cold?"

"Your boss, Lyle, sent us. Said you was over your head out here with bad men and renegades."

"Said I was to help you if I could. Met Phineas here in town. He's Colin's uncle or some relation, I guess. He heard about your trouble and decided to join up with me. Says you can't be trusted to do it by yourself."

"Howdy Phineas. It is good to see you again. I still remember our visit. If I miss my guess, the British have made it hot for you and you skedaddled for a mite."

"Aye, you know me too well from our wee visit, Blackie. I couldn't let a friend of mine do without me company, if he needs ma help. You look well." Both men shook hands.

"Boys, if there's anything ya need, just let me know. I got inventory to tend to. Glad to have you here. Business is still business." Tom exited into the back room, leaving the three men warming against the stove.

"Well, ya gonna tell us what is going on? We come a long way jus to warm up my backsides," Phineas said to no one in particular as he lifted his coattails.

"Yeah, Shep. You don't look frazzled. You look fine. Have you found those renegades, or have you lost them all together?" Quinn inquired.

"Boys, I appreciate Lyle sending you, but I got the leader locked up. Chained to a stable here in the fort, waiting for a judge. Eight dead men laying back on the cutoff. Only one man left and I don't know where he is. I was hoping to spot him, but Tom says he ain't seen nobody that fits his description. If I don't get some lead on him in the next few days, I gotta go and find 'em. It's become a personal issue with me. You boys can escort me if you have a mind. Then my work will be finished here." Shepherd stopped. "Or you can head for home. I gotta stay."

"Don't that beat all? Come all this way just ta say hell-o." Quinn turned his front to the stove. "Looks like he don't need us after all, Stuart."

"Report to the company clerk and he'll see you get assigned to the barracks for the night. I've been invited to supper. Let me go find Bill and see if his wife can feed another couple of hungry men. I'll catch back up to you fellas in the barracks in a few minutes and we'll go eat."

"Aye, that sounds good ta me, Blackie A fine meal cooked by a lady's hand will be a fine thing. I have a wee dram of whiskey I can contribute to the party. Please extend my thanks to Bill's missus, if you please."

"Eh, mine too, Shepherd. I ain't got nuthin' to add to the meal, but I can give some news on what's happening in Salem. That'll be my ticket to the supper." Quinn shouldered his bag and he and Phineas headed to their quarters.

CHAPTER 19

＊◆＊

"That was a fine supper, Frieda. I always have liked elk." Shepherd wiped his face and pushed himself back from the table. "Thank you everyone for your kindness to me and my friends. We will meet up again in Salem, sometime this spring. Stay together and be careful as you're going through the southern mountains. White men have been killing Indians and stealing land. The Indians have had enough and are fighting back. Stay on the trail and you should be fine. There should be militia guarding the roads by now."

The three men said their goodbyes and went out into the cold night. Shepherd had not mentioned the wagon he had found down the trail, at the supper. He did not want to dampen the mood and it was his business to see to. He didn't want to upset the women.

The moon shown as a sliver of silver glow in the blue-black night. It stopped snowing at least for now. No clouds were seen. Cold lay on the land for the first time this season as the dominant predator. Cold was king now. Everybody had to deal with the cold first, when they went out in it. To survive, you had to deal with bone-chilling cold. It was that time of year.

"Aye man, that was a fine supper. I was tired of camp

cooking, though ye be a passable cook, Quinn." Phineas beat his hands together. Steam rose from his face as he spoke. "I hope the stove is warming the barracks this night. I'm due for a bonny night, sleeping in a bed for the first time in months."

"You ain't so bad yourself, when it comes to cooking, Phineas. 'Course, that whiskey would make anything a fine feast. A good night's sleep is just what I hope for too."

"Before you turn in, why don't you come with me and I'll show you Da'vid Angelle, the man I've been telling you about. He's the biggest man I've ever seen, even bigger than any of the Nolans from Indiana, Quinn. I want to make sure he is well locked up. I instructed the attending lieutenant to keep three men watching him at all times. He's as dangerous as a caged bear. I know he'll choke the life out of anyone he can get his hands on."

Shepherd led the way to where he had left Da'vid Angelle in the old stable at the end of the fort. It was dark. They peered into the long building. No lantern, nor torches lit the interior of the stables. Shepherd didn't like it. "Hey. Guard? Anyone here?" Silence answered him back. Shepherd looked at his companions. "This is not good. Quinn, report to the officer on duty and bring him back here with some armed men. Phineas, see if you can put a torch together so we can see. None of us are going in there unless we can see." Shepherd pulled his pistol and made sure his chambers were charged. Phineas lit a couple of torches and handed one to Shepherd. They waited until Quinn returned with more guards.

Quinn arrived accompanied by the officer on duty and three more guards. Shepherd suggested three of the men go around to the back of the stable while the rest approached from the front. Each held torches casting eerie light and shadows as they made their way through the stables. "I never liked fightin' in the dark," Quinn said as they walked. "My daddy used ta tell me to stay out of caves and such and this here reminds me of an old cave."

The flickering light revealed the truth. Three young men lay piled up in the stable. Their necks at odd angles to their bodies. Angelle's shackles were open and lying on top of the three men. "Watch the pitch dripping from your torches, men. We don't want to set the barn on fire."

Lieutenant Ambrose Cane stepped forward to examine the bodies. Shaking his head in pity for the fallen guards, he looked at Shepherd. "All have broken necks. We will assist you in any way we can, Marshal. I must attend to my men first. Would you meet me in my office in the morning and we will confer on what we need to do next. I want the man who crushed the life out of my men." He waved the other guards over. "Pick these men up and take them to the surgery. The post doctor will need to examine them. I know these men, treat them with respect."

Quinn motioned for Shepherd to come to him. He was studying the ground by the door at the rear of the stable, holding a torch high over his head.

"They went out this a way, Shep. Looks like he had some help. Maybe a woman?"

Shepherd knelt down, studying the floor. A smaller boot print next to a much larger one was plainly visible impressed into the soft duff.

"Lonnie! Quinn, that's Angelle's son. They met up again. He was probably waiting for me to show up with his father the whole time. I've got to go after them again. I can't let them get away. It's like keeping a weasel in the henhouse. Everything dies when they are around."

"Lieutenant! Look at this." Shepherd waved to get the lieutenant's attention. "Angelle had help. His son Lonnie probably got the drop on the guards and Angelle finished them quietly, so as not to alarm the fort. I'll be chasing them as soon as we finish with our meeting in the morning."

"I'll send some men with you to assist you, Marshal."

"No. No, thank you, Lieutenant. I work better alone and can move faster."

"We ain't come all this way jist to sit around, whilst you have all the fun, Shepherd," Quinn said as he rose.

"I'm counting on you to come with me," Shepherd said. "You have been deputized. Phineas, you coming, or you sitting this one out? No hard feelings if you do. It's going to be cold and miserable and these men will lead us into Hell's own misery when they realize we are on their trail."

"I am known as Hell's avenger, when I take out after someone myself. Wouldn't miss it. We'll make a fine posse, the three of us. I'll have to tell you da story of how the Scots taught the damn British how to track."

Chapter 20

A fter meeting with the lieutenant in the morning, Shepherd, Quinn, and Phineas circled the fort until they picked up Angelle's and Lonnie's tracks in the hard, crisp snow. Shepherd noted a mule's track as well.

"Lookee here," said Quinn. He examined where the horses had been tied. "They must a had horses waitin' fer them. What's this? A yellow gingham dress? I thought you said Lonnie was his son?"

Shepherd dismounted to examine the dress. "I was sure Lonnie would head this way and was surprised Tom hadn't seen him. Either he used Hannah or he disguised himself as a woman so he could buy supplies without drawing attention. They're headed back toward the cutoff, I think." He folded the dress and placed it in his saddlebag.

"Who's Hannah? You haven't mentioned that name afore now." Quinn watched Shepherd handle the dress.

He noted the curiosity in Quinn's voice as he stuffed the fabric into his saddlebag. "Something I haven't told you yet. While I was bringing in Angelle, I found a wagon with a dead man and woman. I didn't want to spoil supper last night. They were black folks. Their names were Ernest and Pokey Thompson. Both had been tortured, then shot. It had all the markings of Lonnie's doings.

"In their Bible, I found another woman was mentioned. A woman named Hannah. Found her diary hidden in a rag doll. She was a slave and escaped to St. Louis and joined up with the Thompsons. I believe those mule tracks are hers and Lonnie forced her to go with him, or she would have been dead back there as well. Watch who you are shooting at, but I want these men and I want them as much as I have ever wanted to find anyone. Let's go."

Shepherd realized he hadn't told them about Hannah's picture. It seemed like an invasion of her privacy to him, so he just kept quiet. There would be time to tell if needed.

"Got yerself a girlfriend, eh? Dinnae let it drive you, lad. You only need to be a thinking with one head, not two." Phineas rode on. He wasn't making a joke.

Angelle and Lonnie must have moved all night. They had a good long head start. Shepherd was a fair tracker and Quinn was better. To hear Phineas tell it, he was the finest tracker to ever come out of Scotland.

"I once tracked a Indian over a solid granite mountain, and a lake, and was waiting for him when he got to where he was a going."

"How did ya do that?" asked Quinn.

"He was my partner and I knew where he was a going to go to sell the goods he stole from me," replied Phineas with a smirk.

"What did ya do when he showed up?"

"Why, I shot him of course. It is very bad manners to steal from a thief who is your partner. Can never be trusted again."

The tracks were fresh and clear, but the three couldn't make any headway on catching up to the fugitives. In a few days, Names Hill loomed ahead of them.

That evening, Shepherd read from the journal: *"Pokey is trying to teach me to knit. My fingers are so thick, I don't think I will be able to do it. Sunshine in the morning, rainy and cloudy later in the day. Mush and bacon for breakfast.*

Earnest shot a groundhog and we had a fine supper."

"I knew it," Shepherd told them. "They're headed back to the old store with the red angel on top. Old dogs revert back to old habits." Shepherd looked over his shoulder. A tiny speck was visible on the horizon. "Someone is following us. Once we go over this next rise, let's pull off and see who's coming. I don't like trouble on both ends of my trail."

They moved over the rise and waited on their horses under some old junipers. Hoof clops sounded on the other side of the hill and then a head and a body. Burro walked up to Shepherd's foot and scratched his neck on his stirrup.

"Burro!" Shepherd laughed out loud. "What are you doing here? Quinn, Phineas, meet Burro. He has saved my life a time or two. I owe him. Sorry, I forgot all about you, little fella. I guess you're going with us." Shepherd dismounted to rub between his ears and neck.

"Well, Shepherd. If'n ya don't mind, we need to get back to business. Give your burro a little kiss and let's get back to work, if'n you don't mind." Quinn had a big grin on his face. "I know how lonely a man can get out here, but, Shepherd, your girlfriend surprises me how pretty she looks!"

"Ha ha, you fellas. Burro is a he, and he and I just became buddies while I was hunting down Angelle and his gang. He did save my life more than once. I forgot about him back there and he followed me."

"Whar I come from, that's illegal, me boy," Phineas said.

He and Quinn hooted and rode on laughing to each other.

"We'll show them, won't we, Burro." Shepherd dug a peppermint candy out of his pocket and fed it to his friend. "Stay up with us. We've got a long way to go."

Crossing the Green River in the cold was treacherous. The water was high and rimmed with sharp ice. The horses struggled to get up the bank, but Burro leapt on ahead and waited on top of the ridge.

"Maybe, Burro may come to some good after all, Shepherd. Think we could put some packs on him and lighten the pack mule's load?"

"After what you said about him? I don't think so, Quinn."

"Ah, Shep, we was just a joshing ya. Ya know that."

"I know, Quinn. I think Burro has won a reprieve for a little while at least, after the mean things you said. I'm just going to let him be for now. We're headed that way." He pointed toward the cutoff.

"I don think so, Blackie. Look at what I'm lookin' at."

"Damn it." Quinn spit into the snow as he looked to where Phineas pointed. Tracks of a large horse and a smaller one, followed by a mule, then two pack animals were headed north up the Green. Their tracks left little doubt who they were. No other signs led to the cutoff or made their way north along the Green.

"Lonnie has her tethered pretty tight to him by the looks of it. What's that mean, Quinn? They're headed north? What's up that way?" Shepherd studied the tracks. His stomach lurched under his belt and his mouth went dry. Disappointment and confusion overwhelmed him. Hannah felt farther and farther away.

Quinn danced his horse around as he got his bearings. "Yellowstone, maybe that hole in the mountains. They're headed north to sit out the winter in one of the mostest peculiar parts of the world I ever did see."

"I've heard of Yellowstone," mused Phineas. "Many a man is rumored to have stayed the winter close to those hot springs. They's buffalo and elk up there. A man can sit in a hot stone tub and roast buffalo tongue by the fire and dip hot water out of a spring ta make his coffee or tea. An enchanted place, I hear." Phineas cut off a piece of jerky. Chewing it for a while, he washed it down with a taste of his bottle. "Wouldn't mind seeing this place if that is where you want to go."

Shepherd looked to the north, mulling the possibilities in his mind. "I've heard of Yellowstone too."

Quinn said, "Some say it's haunted by old Indian spirits. Hot geysers shooting hundreds of feet into the air, falling back to earth in the wintertime as sharp ice splinters, able to cut a man to shreds. Frozen rivers and painted springs of blue and green waters."

"That's where they're headed?" Shepherd looked to the mountains.

"Appears to me they are." Quinn crossed his arms over his saddle horn. "Much worse than traveling in the desert, this time of year. No one goes to the mountains in the wintertime, after the big snows. They's heading to Yellowstone, maybe Jackson's Hole, but my guess is Yellowstone. The Hole gets closed in with snow, but if they get in there before it snows deep, we've lost 'em. May as well turn back now. I think Yellowstone. Too late ta get in the Hole."

"Don't know either way, Blackie, but I'm with you whatever way you decide," Phineas said.

"I've always wanted to see Yellowstone." Shepherd led the way following the deteriorating tracks in the snow north, leaving crunching noises in the still-frigid air. He wasn't giving up now.

They came to the Mormon crossing. Shepherd was remembered by the brethren, and welcomed. "Yes, they had seen the pair. They did meet with the leader. One giant of a man and one much smaller. They traded horses, bought some supplies, and headed off over a day ago. Seemed to be in a hurry. Said they were going north to trap through the winter. Didn't say where. Paid with cash money. No one saw any traps. No. No woman was with them."

"Once they leave the Green River, there's no telling where they might go. The two of them can kill a buff or take a few elk and live mighty good next to a hot spring up there. Ground shakes with earthquakes pretty often. Scare the pants off of ya, the first time ya feel it." Quinn studied the tracks after they left the Mormon enclave. "Packhorses is loaded pretty fair. Mule is doing fair. They will slow down in the snow of the high country. We should catch them on the Teton front, at the pace we're a goin'."

"Then let's get moving. Phineas, you been in this country before?"

"Naw, man. Not in snow and cold like this." Phineas rubbed his hands together, looking north at the line of departing tracks. "They mus' be desperate ta go up thar dis time of year."

"They are. I already killed eight of the gang. I found most of the money they stole and they know I'm coming after 'em. Then, there's the woman. They don't know I know about her. I thought they'd head for Angelle's store, but they must have figured the same thing. North is their only chance to get away and they got Hannah. I saw what they did to the Thompsons. They may be using her in case they need a hostage." Shepherd looked to Quinn, hoping he'd give him some reassurance she would be all right.

"I hope she minds her manners, 'cause if she becomes a burden, they'll kill her for sure." Quinn stood in his stirrups and looked up the trail. "At least they broke trail for us. Their horses is working almighty hard. We should catch them. Let's go. Take turns riding point."

Quinn moved to lead the way. Snow was just over the horses' hooves as they sprayed snow with each step. Wind was coming out of the passes from the north, working down steep dusty slopes into their faces. Flecks of snow laced the wind and danced in small fluffy flakes.

It wasn't too bad…yet.

CHAPTER 21

ater that day, Phineas was leading the party when he stopped and got off his horse to brush the snow off of a mound alongside the trail. "It's one of their packhorses," he called and waved for them to come see. "Looks ta broke leg. At least they put the poor creature outa its misery. Didn't even unpack her. They know we are on their trail."

"Let's take a breather ourselves," Quinn said. "We've been pushing since morning. We don't wanna make the same mistakes. I could use some coffee. Phineas, rummage through their packs and see if'n there's anythin' we can use." He pointed to the dead animal. "Shepherd and me will make camp." Quinn found a sheltered place in the rocks and began breaking sticks from dead branches of spruce and pine to make a fire.

Shepherd led the horses into a copse of rocks and trees then tethered them out of the wind. He pulled off the saddles and packs to give the animals some relief but left their blankets. He threw a blanket over Burro and gave them all a bait of corn and oats.

Feeling the higher elevation, he blew puffs of vapor. The sky was starkly clear blue with trailing wisps of clouds far overhead. He wasn't happy that Angelle and Lonnie had headed north. It made more work for him and his posse, but that was the job they had set out to do.

The woman, Hannah, had not left his mind since he found the Thompsons. Gratefully, he extended his hands toward Quinn's fire. "We've made good time, thanks to their broken trail. How much have we made up, Quinn?"

"A few hours, I figure. They'll panic, now that they've killed the packhorse and lost half of their supplies. They're running harder now trying to keep ahead. We'll rest here for the night. It's about an hour before dark. No sense killing ourselves in the cold and darkness. We're catching up. They will keep going after dark, trying to get ahead. Yes sir, they going to wear themselves down to a nub. End up killing themselves."

"'Ere's some more blankets and food. I cut some nice steaks from the horse. No sense leavin' good meat. We'll eat good tonight, I'm a guessin. If we can keep the wind off of us. Does it ever stop blowin'?" Phineas hunkered down on his haunches and poured himself some coffee. "I don't think I'd wanna be those fellas tonight. Wind is pickin' up. After pullin' off the packs, I dragged the animal about a mile back down the trail so's the wolves won't bother us."

"We should cache the supplies we can't use." He pointed to the loose strewn about. "Might come in useful on our way back to have them. We can make a rock cairn to keep the wolves out. Something on top of the ground so we don't have to dig. Ground is pretty frozen. It will serve to block the wind tonight for the rest of us and make a good reflector."

"You're the boss, Blackie. I dinnae like the idea of starvin' myself. A cold bleak world out here, it is. Reminds me of the Highlands of home."

They piled up rocks to block the wind and make the cairn. Then filled the void with the supplies they found. They stacked logs and boulders to keep the cache secure from wolves and wolverines.

Shepherd laid the gingham dress over the top weighted down with rocks. "It'll help us find it if it snows." Camp was placed in front of a dusty cliff face with the fire built up in front of the rock wall. The rock cairn was at a ninety-degree angle to the rock face. Both reflected heat and light back on them and against the cliff. Phineas showed them how to build a fire that would last through the night, the way he had learned to do it in the Highlands. Horsemeat cooked on the coals, with beans heated in its can, and bannock wrapped around a stick was their supper. Canned peaches for dessert.

Phineas hummed Scottish ditties to himself as he worked around and tended the fire, He fussed around and fixed the fire the way he wanted it, then pulled a bottle from beneath his bedroll. They hunkered underneath thick coats and blankets basking in the warmth of their fire. Phineas took a pull then passed it to Quinn, who saluted Phineas and passed it to Shepherd.

Their heads sunk in silence as light burst out in one last gasp of brilliance before the sun sunk behind the mountains casting long shadows on those firelit faces, each lost in their own thoughts, gazing into the popping fire, resigned to the journey in the morning. Phineas continued humming, occasionally breaking out in song in Gaelic. No one minded.

Off in the distance, howls droned into the night, followed by more and more mournful yips and a yowling chorus. "Wolves found the horse, I reckon." Quinn took a swallow of the bottle. "Sends chilblains down mah back every time I hear that."

"Aye. Wish I had brought me dudlesack." Phineas pulled his collar high over his head.

"What's a dudlesack?" Quinn passed the bottle off to Shepherd then scooched down into his blankets, staring into the fire.

"You would call it bagpipes, Quinn. Dudlesack is an

old, old word for bagpipes. Have a heart, Blackie, pass dat bottle. I feel your melancholy."

"Oh, here." Shepherd passed the bottle over to Phineas. He had been brooding about Hannah, staring into the flames. "Lost in thought, I guess. Thanks for the drink." He pulled the sachet out of his pocket and held it to his nose as he pulled his collar up over his ears with his other hand. His eyes searched up the distant trail.

Phineas noticed the distress on his face and patted him on his back. "Get some sleep, my friend. What's going on out there is beyond your control. Do what you can, but don' dwell on it. It can drive a man crazy. I know."

CHAPTER 22

⟡

S he was right there within his reach. He couldn't see her face, but it was Hannah. He reached for her. He started falling. It didn't frighten him, just perplexed him. How he could be so close and still not touch her?

Shepherd bounced in his blankets as he thumped back into reality from his vivid dream. He felt a scratching on his belly and it was moving up to his face. A mouse poked its nose out of his blankets, twitching its whiskers. "Dag nab it." He sat and brushed the small creature away from him into a snowbank, where it burrowed out of sight.

Quinn threw a stick of wood on the fire, looking up at Shepherd's startled expression. "Seems you had company in your dreams last night. I had a mouse or two myself I had to throw outta ma blankets. Hope they don't destroy our supply cache. Coffee?"

Morning sunshine lit the valley they camped in, with a million refracted, reflections of light that made them squint to keep their eyes from hurting. Puffs of breath condensed in the air as the men moved about, stretched stiff cramped muscles, and rubbed sore places on their arms and necks. It was a morning to make spirits lift and a body be thankful they had been born. A morning that called for hot coffee to mellow your thoughts and set your mind for the day. Cold crisp air bit the men's faces and chilled the exposed parts of their bodies. They had kept warm last night as they moved around, taking turns, performing camp duties.

This morning, Quinn's hot coffee fueled their work as they readied the horses. They packed their bedrolls and gulped down the rest of the fresh meat Quinn cooked over the coals.

Shepherd squatted on his heels and wondered at the beauty around him. Gooseflesh moved up his back in appreciation of the morning, bursting with the light of a thousand crystal chandeliers. Cold air crackled above them with the crunch of frozen snow on every step.

Occasionally, during his travels, he turned inward on the magnificence of where he was, and the immensity of the country surrounding which left him in awe. He looked back on where he came from and his place in it and bowed his head in grateful appreciation, sucked in some cold air, and slowly savored the steaming coffee in his cup. Reluctantly, his thoughts turned back to the task at hand. The beauty around him faded. He rose and began lashing his bedroll to his saddle. He wondered what Hannah's morning was like.

"Whatcha waiting for, Quinn? I think we catch up to them today." Phineas mounted his horse and snugged up the reins of his pack animal.

"I think so too, Phineas. I figure by midafternoon, we should spot them at the pace we've been setting. A woman always slows a man's progress. My guess is they'll be regretful they took her. A man don't always do what's in his own best interest sometimes."

"That would be lucky for us. Shep, I's suspect you'll get to meet this woman you're all worked up about when we do catch up. Hope you ain't disappointed." Quinn grinned at Shepherd's embarrassment, as he led the way up the trail. Phineas and Shepherd followed and Burro took up from behind.

The men didn't break for the noon hour. They chose to move steadily on, not taxing the horses as they followed the track through the brilliant sunshine and crisp, even snow. By midafternoon, they saw three dark shadows disappearing over a ridge a few miles ahead.

"Do ya think they saw us, Quinn?" Phineas had pulled over behind some bare birch trees, trying to get out of sight.

"I don't know, Phineas. We'll see what their tracks say when we get to where they were. That will tell for sure." Quinn looked around the trees to see if the trail was clear. "Let's move on ahead here. Keep the horses quiet. We don't want to alert them; a fair rifle shot could pick anyone off from here."

A sharp crack echoed between the mountain ridges. In that moment, a branch tore off just over Phinehas's head and fell on his shoulders and back. He instinctively ducked at the noise. "My guess is, they have seen us." He backed his horse farther off the trail and pulled the still-quivering branch off of his back. "Damnation that was close."

Shepherd pulled up Dusty, put the smooth cold stock of his rifle to his right cheek, breathed a deep breath, steadied, and fired an answering shot at the retreating figures, who hurriedly sped up and disappeared. "Can't say I hit anybody. But they do know we are coming. Let's go." Clucking to his horse, he started up the trail toward the now-empty cleft in the forest.

Quinn took off next, followed by Phineas. Their horses were fresh, relishing the chance to run and stretch their muscles. The running warmed them and broke the monotony of the slow, steady pace they had been making.

Shepherd signaled a halt as they approached where the gang had tried to bushwhack them. Quinn moved up to observe the trail.

"They're running now. We haven't let them stop for food or rest all day. We can't get too close fer fear they'll take another shot at us. If we stay too far back, we might lose them. What do you want to do, Marshal?"

"We stay on their tail, driving them on until something gives. The pressure is on them. Let's see if something blows. My bet is they'll leave the woman."

The posse followed the tracks that took them deeper into the mountains. Careful of each turn they took, lest a rife bullet was waiting for them. Crossing a tumbling stream, the three crept closer and closer to their prey, knowing Angelle and Lonnie would turn like any feral creature, willing to fight to the death to keep their lives, no matter the odds.

"Look up there!" Quinn pointed up a rocky slope to a small shack, where the jagged line of tracks in the snow ended. "We've brought them to bay. Problem is, they have a clean shot in any direction." White smoke swirled out of the smokestack whipped by the winds.

"They'll be nice and warm at least. Which is more than we can say for ourselves down here, a lookin' up at them. What'll we do, Quinn?" Phineas had gotten off of his horse, removed his gloves, and was blowing on his hands, looking up the canyon over the top of his saddle.

"I say we have to wait. Not many more hours until the sun goes down. What say, Marshal? We wait, or we go?"

"Let's not let them be so comfortable. You boys go on down around that last bend and set us up a good camp. No telling how long we gonna be here. I'm going to let them know we're here. I don't want them too comfortable. How's your powder and ball? I'm gonna pepper the shack. They can't hit me if I'm behind these rocks. They can't come down and we can't go up." Shepherd tied Dusty to a spruce limb and started climbing up the trail.

Two shots rang out, dusting snow in the trees over his head. Shepherd ducked and crawled on his belly to a boulder off to the left of the trail. "They haven't figured out how to shoot downhill yet," he called back to them. "Go on. I'm fine. Gonna keep them busy for a while." He fired high into the front door. Then into each of the two windows, again, high enough to miss anyone behind them.

His thoughts reminded him, *"Don't shoot at the girl."* Return shots ricocheted off the rocks around him. Nothing came close. He moved his position. If he stayed low enough, they couldn't see his movement until he fired again.

For the next two hours, Shepherd hid and moved through the rock field below the shack, picking his targets. He shattered the windows, leaving only large shards hanging in the panes then peppered the smokestack until it bent over itself and hung despondently over the wooden cabin, still buoyed up by the small cables that had held it upright. A few shots were returned from the shack. All shots from the cabin were in vain, as he moved after each shot.

Red sunlight glinted on the remaining splinters of glass before the sun winked itself off for the night. Then all was blackness, except for a low glow behind the door and windows of the tiny refuge, which must have come from a stove or fire they had going to keep themselves from freezing.

Shepherd found Dusty and carefully picked his way in the dark, back down to the camp where the other two were waiting. He rubbed the horse down, gave him a nosebag of food, and covered him with a blanket and made sure Burro had something to eat, before joining the other men at the welcoming fire.

"We keep them from sleeping, if we take turns taking potshots at the shack all night. Just a random shot here and there, enough to disturb and keep them from sleeping. Holler and yip like a bunch of Indians. Call out to each other as if we were going to attack at any time. We can take turns sleeping and shooting throughout the night. A trick Jon and I learned from the Indians."

"Sounds good ta me. I'll take the first watch. Every

three hours did you say?" Phineas turned his back and disappeared into the blackness. The crunch of his footsteps as they faded away gave the only indication he was there at all, just a lonely sound in the silence. Soon, a lonely shot echoed in the still night. A few minutes later, another. No one in the cabin would sleep.

Shepherd sat down next to the fire watching the popping spruce logs glowing orange and blue. He pulled his blankets over his shoulders. Spooning some of the simmering stew into his tin cup, he blew softly, until it was cool enough to eat, then chewed each mouthful in deep thought. When he was finished, he pulled his blankets over his shoulders, wrapping them around him. He slept until Quinn woke him to continue their haranguing of the shack.

CHAPTER 23

N ext morning, Shepherd ordered his men to spread out for the attack. They brought up their mounts in case they needed to move fast. The front of the shack was pockmarked with bright splinters of wood against the dark veneer of the shanty's patina. The door hung at an odd angle. Some of the glass was starred in the panes, giving the poor cabin the appearance of a blind apparition.

Shepherd fired above the left window. No response. He fired above the door. No response. He waved his arm to Phineas to move closer. Still no response. Moving slowly from rock to rock, he called into the shack. "Angelle, Lonnie, come out! There's no place for you to go. Come out now. Lonnie. Come out! We'll show you no mercy if we have to fight our way in. Come out with your hands empty."

Quiet descended on the mountaintop. Shep indicated for Quinn to check the back of the cabin. He and Phineas slowly climbed the steps of the porch. Prickles of apprehension shown on their faces.

Quinn came around from behind the cabin, his rifle dangling from his hand. "No use, Shep. They've gone. No horses in the back stable not even the mule. There's a trail leading to a small saddle going over the mountain. They must have taken off sometime before daylight. No one is here."

"Stand back, Phineas, I'm goin' in."

Shepherd pushed open the door. Inside was a jumble of broken lamps and scattered tinware. A small stove at the back of the one-room shack still glowed, with wood stacked along one wall. The remains of a meal were on the table. Three plates were set. A cold pot of overturned stew and a pan of cornbread lay spilled on the floor. An empty liquor bottle lay under one of the windows. Sunlight shone through the holes shot in the walls. The place was pretty wrecked, but no sign of Angelle or Lonnie. A pile of clothes lay on the bed. Women's clothes. Shepherd bent over and pulled a torn blue gingham dress off of the top, similar to the one now guarding their food cache back down the trail.

"Yaaaa!" A knife flashed out of the pile, scarcely missing Shepherd's face. The pile exploded with a body holding a very bright and sharp knife. "Hecate's wrath, twist your innards into knots and you will shriek with agony. You will scream like the fires of hell are bound to your guts!"

A black woman stood on the bed clad in rags with hair twisted into braided knots, tied with ribbons and pieces of cloth. Wild staring eyes faced them. She threatened them each time one of them moved. Her sharp knife passed from hand to hand. The woman hissed under her breath, growling deep and low like a cornered animal.

"Now calm down, missy." Phineas held out his hand in supplication.

"More damn men!" she shrieked. "Damn all men to hell." She leapt to the floor and fell on her knees, scrambling herself up in an instant, keeping the hot stove to her back. She drew the flat side of the blade effortlessly across her tongue. "Who will be the first to die? I will drink your blood and rip your bowels out of your bodies and feed them to pigs!" Again, she moved the knife back and forth between her hands, inviting them to come to her then feinting attack, muttering chants that made no sense to the men.

"I believe she is mad, Shepherd. We should leave her. Der's nothing we can do for her." Phineas crossed himself.

"Stars and night! I beg for your blood when the moon be bright." Her wild eyes darted from one to the other. "Pan's bride by day and Hecate's mistress at night. Touch me and thee truly will die." Stabbing at them, she laughed a maniacal laugh. "Hsssss." She crept behind the stove, shifting from side to side guarding her space. She thrust the knife in their direction, baring her teeth. She hissed and spat. "Damn men, damn them all to burning hell."

Shepherd laid his gun on the table and held his hands up, palms open. Sweat ran down his face and the prickles of his neck screamed a warning! *Is this Hannah? What the hell?*

His voice cracked when he spoke, "We have come to help you, Miss. Let us help you." He stepped over to the stove, palms up. "Please, Hannah, we are here to help."

Recognition of her name registered on her face for an instant. Sneering at him, she stabbed down at his leg, and then flashed up like she would eviscerate him from his crotch to his throat. "Don't cha touch me, field hand! I am a white man's woman. I don't take up with no common field boys." Hysterical laughter erupted from her chest as she leaned over and picked up the bucket of ashes and flung them with a sweeping motion over all three men. Shrieking her curses, she ran out the door and down the trail out of sight.

Sputtering and gasping for breath, Quinn, Phineas, and Shepherd came out on the porch, white with ash, brushing themselves off and wiping their eyes and faces.

"Gotta wash des ashes off or they burn your skin,"

gasped Quinn. "Shake out your clothes too. Nothin' more sore-some than blisters around your waist and nether parts." Reluctantly, they had to strip off their clothes and shake them off outside in the brilliant intense cold. Using snow to bathe in, they cleaned themselves.

"Just dust yourself with the snow. If it melts, wipe it off. Ashes and water make lye. It'll burn ya sure as you're born." Embarrassed, they avoided looking at each other. "Better put on your other set of clothes, until you can wash these others. They'll blister ya for sure."

Phineas's white skinny body hop stepped to his packhorse. "Hold on there, Jack. It's just me. I ain't no dad-blamed ghost. Don't step on me." He retrieved his clothes like the others. Sitting on the porch, he pulled on his pants only looking up when a piercing maniacal laughter resounded up the trail. "Ya think she saw us necked?" An eerie cackling laugh echoed across the ravines and snow-filled valleys. "Maybe so. I ain't as purdy as I was when I was young."

"She stopped us for sure. I'd ruther been shot." Quinn pulled on his boots after wiping them with snow and pounding them until the ash was all out.

"Now what do I do? Angelle and Lonnie are gone... headed north up the mountain. There's a half-naked crazy woman running loose, I feel responsible for. She's going the other way down the mountain. I think I'm more afraid of her than the Angelles." Shepherd pulled on his boots, glancing down the trail in the direction the crazy witch had run.

"She's got my spine hackles a tingling that's for sure. I'll go after Angelle and his spawn if it pleases you. I dinnae want nothin' more to do with the witch woman. White or black, I want no part of her. Did I ever tell you I was married to a witch? Best be careful, Shepherd. They ain't to be trifled with. She'll cut out your heart in a minute. Watch yer back." Phineas moved over to adjust the cinch on his horse.

"I don't know 'bout no witches, like Phineas here, but I have seen voo doo oncet, when I was in New Orleans, tried to raise the dead. I didn't care fer it myself, but it seemed to please a lot of them there. Stay here an see what yer can do fer her, Shepherd. If'n you can find her. She's goin' ta freeze fer sure if ya don't. Phineas and I will find Angelle and Lonnie. Damn, I thought we had 'em too. We'll be back when we finish."

Quinn and Phineas mounted and reined their horses and made for the trail at the rear of the shack. "I fer one, ere relieved to have only murderers and thieves to worry about," Phineas shouted to Quinn as he turned down the trail in pursuit of Lonnie and Angelle.

Shepherd watched them disappear around the back of the house. Turning in exasperation, he cast his eyes down the trail. Small bare footprints ran down through the rocks and snow. His stomach churned. After a hundred feet, there was blood in the prints. They moved off of the trail and down a sharp ravine heading for a gushing stream bubbling and splashing down the mountain side. It was loud.

His call was shrill in his throat. "Hannah! Hannah!" There was no answer. "Hannah. Hannah." No answer. By now, the running stream was so loud he couldn't have heard if she did call back.

The tracks led downstream where the water splashed upon the rocks, covering them in slick clear ice. A glimpse of blue caught his eye. He found her face down in the water. Her arms stretched out over her shoulders as if she had flung herself into the rushing stream. The only reason she hadn't been washed away was the splash of cloth he had seen had wedged between some rocks. Pulling on her clothes to bring her to him, he slipped on the ice into water up to his knees. Stumbling to keep his feet under him in the rushing water, he was drenched to his waist.

Somehow, he had kept her head above and out of the

icy tumbling stream. Gritting his teeth, he inched backward against the flowing current that was lapping up his back and nudging him downstream. He kept his balance by digging his boots in between rocks. Grasping her to him, he struggled against the current, until he managed to sit on some small boulders and roll her over onto the bank to his left.

Shepherd pulled himself out of the water. His feet numb and his body shivering, his clothes were starting to freeze to his body. He fought to stand. Picking Hannah up in his arms, her clothes were already adhering to the rocks she lay on, and he had to jerk her free of the stream's freezing grasp. Clutching her to him, he stood and walked a few steps back up the trail, looking at her face. He shook her briefly, took her face in his hands, rubbing her cold cheeks to revive her. There was no response. He laid her over his knee and slapped her back twice sharply. Water erupted from her mouth and she sucked in the cold air. Immediately, she went into violent tremors.

Shewas shaking all over.

Shepherd took off his wool coat and wrapped her in it then picked her up and ran back to the cabin without dropping her. He held the poor trembling woman clasped tightly to him. She weighed nothing.

Why this woman moved him so, he could not understand.

He stripped her wet clothes off of her and bundled her into the bed, wrapping clothes and anything he could find to warm her. Stoking the fire, he added wood. Finding a kettle behind the stove, he filled it with snow and put it on the boil.

Cold wind rattled the door open, flaring the brim of his hat, raising the flesh on his back and legs, reminding him how wet he was.

Shepherd slammed the door closed, jamming it tight in the frame. Stripping off his clothes for the second time that day, he wrapped a blanket around himself. Bracing the door with a bench to keep it tight as possible, he filled the holes in the walls and windows with whatever he could find then went around poking something into every bullet hole he could see.

His fingers failed him. He had to use the barrel of his pistol to push bits into the holes. With repeated jamming sticks, bits of cloth, anything he could find to block the wind and cold in the remaining holes.

Hanging his clothes to dry on a chair close to the stove, he looked around for anything that needed to be done. Finding a crate, he sat next to the stove, thrusting his feet and hands toward the fire. He jerked them back again as the blood painfully returned. He warmed his feet and hands until they worked again and he could slap some circulation into them.

Satisfied, he added more wood and went to check Hannah. Her face was frightening pale and blue around her lips. His hands found her cheeks and lips cold, but he could feel a heartbeat and she was breathing. Gently wiping the makeup off her face, he got a chance to look at her for the first time. Her beauty under the ghoulish mask caught him by surprise.

Trying to take his mind off of her, he rubbed her hands and feet to bring circulation back into them, but the trembling would not stop. He realized he was trembling as much as she, but he was no longer trembling from cold. The only thing he knew to do would be to slide into bed with her and warm her, himself. "You ain't no witch woman, no matter how much you tried to scare us. I refuse to believe that."

She was a mystery he couldn't figure out. "All right, crazy woman, here I come. It's the best I know how to do. Nothing personal." He unwrapped his blankets pulling them around her then moved up against her back and icy thighs, finally wrapping his arms around her in a warming embrace. He held her, until her breath came regularly and the trembling stopped. She slept in his arms. He turned her so he could warm her other side.

"Okay, Shepherd, don think about what you're doing. Just get her warm. Keep your eyes up here and just let her get warm. You can explain in the morning." Feeling strangely affectionate, he snuggled up against her. The affectionate feeling didn't last long and he began to feel a certain pleasant discomfort he hadn't felt in a long time.

"No time for that, boy!" He admonished himself. He would have enjoyed the feeling if it would have been reciprocated. Something deep within him knew she was a wounded creature. Nothing he could ever say or do would be forgiven if he took advantage of this moment. He rewrapped a blanket around his waist so he wasn't touching her skin to skin. In a few minutes, he fell asleep with his lips next to her neck, her breath coming in short puffs against his chest.

He awoke with a start in the dark night. The stove was dim. Stepping out of the warm bed, he pulled on dry pants, then shirt, and finally some dry socks. He stoked the fire and added more wood, which caught and burned brightly, casting shadows around the cabin. The kettle had boiled down and he refilled it.

Finding an oil lamp that still survived, he nursed a tiny flame from the wick and set the glass chimney over the top. Throwing his coat over his back he went outside to see to the horses and get them fed. He brought back supplies, retrieving some coffee and bacon, an onion, and a couple of potatoes. It was blowing. Winds were coming from the north. It felt like snow outside. This shack was going to have to do.

He swept the debris back along the wall so it was safe to walk around. The kettle was steaming as he poured boiling water over the coffee and stirred it a few times and let the grounds settle while he carved some bacon and set it to frying. He cut up the potatoes and onions, ready to fry in the grease when the bacon was done.

Wind blew the door open. He quickly shut it and braced the fallen bench under the handle at a better angle.

More snow was coming, he could tell for certain, from the way the wind smelled. In these higher elevations, it could snow several feet deep in a few hours. The aroma of frying bacon and brewing coffee wafted to his nose. He hadn't eaten all day and his stomach knew it.

Hannah slept, thrashing about, muttering under her breath. She lay still after a while, lightly snoring. The sound of her sleeping reassured Shepherd, bringing some peace of mind to him, and a smile forced its way onto his face while he watched her. He worried about her, but she appeared to be deeply asleep. He breathed a sigh of contentment.

He sipped his coffee and felt a pang of guilty concern for his friends. *How were Quinn and Phineas doing?*

CHAPTER 24

⋄•◦✦◦•⋄

"I tell ya, Quinn, I feel like a damn fool, letting that woman scare me into running off like that. Just too many memories from my ol' wife came flooding back in my mind. Now ere we are on top of a damnable mountain and snow clouds billowing all around us. Damn, we need to get out of this weather."

"I feel the same way, Phineas. We shoulda waited, but we was hot on their trail and truth be told, she gave me the willies. I'm tired of this hunt. I want it over. We need cover, damn good cover, and fast. It's a fixin' to blizzard and I don't want to be left out in deep snow."

"Aye, I'm a looking for a thick copse of trees for cover, an overhang of some kind in da rocks, anythin' ta break the wind and give us some shelter. See anything' that we could use, Quinn?" Phineas scanned the rocky outcroppings around them. Thick, gray clouds scudded through the mountains, threatening to release their heavy snow.

"I've been looking for the last several miles and ain't seen nuthing yet. Maybe something around this next bend. Look up and down for something, anything." The wind gusted and blew at Quinn's hat. He had to quickly grab it. Tying his scarf around the top of his head, he secured his hat good and tight.

"What's that? Look up there, Quinn, behind that stand of spruce up on da mountainside. The wind blew the branches and I thought I saw a black opening. There. Did you see?"

"I do, Phineas. Good eye. You want to climb up there and look or I'll do it."

"I saw it. I'll go. C'mon, horsey, up ya go." Phineas zigzagged up the incline, and he and Danny Boy disappeared into the stand of spruces about a hundred feet up from the trail.

Quinn held the packhorse, watching for any signal from the copse of trees. After what seemed to be forever, Phineas rode out from the beneath the skirts of spruces and waved his hat to come on up.

Carefully, Quinn followed Phineas' path up the steep incline. It would not do to break an animal's leg or fall onto these sharp rocks.

"What did ya find?"

"I'm not too sure. Come see for yourself." Phineas broke off some dead spruce knots and tied them tightly together to use as a torch. He waved for Quinn to follow. After tying the horses, the men entered the pitch-black cleft in the rocks. It appeared like a crack in the mountain. They followed the cleft until the sides of the walls fell away into a larger opening.

Quinn grabbed Phineas' arm to keep him from going farther. "Better light your torch here. You never know what is under your nex' step. We don' want to come upon any sleepin' bears either."

Out of the wind, Phineas struck iron and pyrite together to make a spark. He directed his efforts toward a pile of duff he had collected off of the floor to catch the spark. Carefully, he nursed an ember to life and gave that life, more life, by adding splinters of shaved spruce until it caught the vapor and became fire. He touched his torch of spruce knots to those flames and holding the torch aloft, looked about the room.

"My word, Phineas, what have we here?"

Phineas' torch illuminated a large room about forty feet across and ten feet high. Dark passage ways radiated off from this central room in three different directions. Sand covered the floor. An old black-sooted fire ring was centered in the room. Piles of brush and smaller logs for firewood were stacked against one wall. Logs for sitting were placed around the fire ring.

Quinn kneeled and sifted the bits of charcoal between his fingers, smelling the bits as he did so. "Someone has had a fire here not long ago. Almos' looks like we was expected. Don' look a gift of any kind in the eye, my daddy always said. Let's get the horses and make a fire."

"Snowing," said Phineas as they moved outside. Wind whipped the spruce branches around in a frenzy.

"Yep. Expected it." Quinn moved all the horses to the back of the room and tethered them together, then he fed them. Tossing wood from the nearby stacks into the charred ring, Phineas used his sputtering torch to light a fire. "Whatever spirits is lookin' out over us, I thank ye." He held his hat over his heart as he spoke. Both men, he realized, were overwhelmed at their good luck in finding this place. Facing a night outdoors with a blizzard blowing was facing a cold and untimely death this time of year. They went out to gather whatever branches and dead wood they could find. Everything was buried under feet of drifting snow. They cut spruce boughs for sleeping beds and dragged dead and green logs inside the cave to cut up as needed.

The room was warming up, and it was a relief to be out of the wind after they had finished. Phineas put on some coffee, spread his blankets, and took off his boots. "That feels good on me feet. My toes was about froze off. How long do ya think we'll be here, Quinn?"

Quinn pulled his coat closer around his shoulders. This place gave him the willies. "Don' know. Several days, maybe. We got lucky finding this cave. Must have been used for some type of ceremonies by the Indians or somethin', by the looks of it. Maybe an old trapper used it for a hidey hole. Look around after we eat, if you want. We got to make our fuel last for as long as possible. The wood along the walls is good, but it's way dry. It will burn fast. Once these rocks we piled up around the fire get heated up, they should hold some of the heat. We'll sleep good tonight.

"I'll start supper. Oysters and quail for you tonight?" He smiled as he held up some pemmican and jerky.

Phineas looked up. "Oh boy, I ain't had oysters in a long time."

"Stew, then?" Quinn smiled.

"Stew sounds good too." Phineas smiled at their little joke. They would need a sense of humor in the coming days. He was glad Quinn was a good camp mate.

Phineas melted snow then chopped up pemmican and a chunk of dried vegetables, added some powdered soup, and stirred it with a stick. Setting it close to the fire to cook, he poured some coffee, passed a cup to Quinn, and waited for the stew to boil. "Don't we have some flour somewhere? I make the best bannock this side of Aberdeen. It'll go good with the soup."

He got up to search the packs and came away with what he was looking for, flour and a bottle.

He went down the cleft opening to the entrance and poked his head out of the cave to see heavy snow drifting down in huge fluffy flakes.

"It's as cold as me second wife out dar," Phineas said when he came back. He set himself down and began mixing his bannock, whistling a low tune.

"I hope never to meet the poor woman, then. How many wives have you had, Phineas?"

"That question my friend, is always open for conjecture. Les just say, I's had my share." He poured water over his flour, added salt, saleratus, and some back fat, and mixed it up with his hands until the dough was no longer sticky. Then he wrapped it around a smooth branch, stripped free of bark, and propped it over the fire to bake. "Supper will be ready, a' for ya know it." Satisfied with his work, he slurped his coffee and watched his bread bake over the glowing coals and sipped at a small glass of whiskey sitting beside him, firelight glinting off of the amber liquid through the crystal.

"Where do you think these tunnels lead?" Phineas pointed to the other shafts radiating out from the central room as they stood by the fire, warming their hands and legs.

"My guess is somebody's been mining in here. From the shape of it, a long time ago. They's no wind blowing in to blow our fire, so there's no outside opening. Want to take a look down one of the shafts?" Quinn bent down on one knee by the fire, stirring the stew in the pot.

"Dinae dat I do. Holes in the ground worry me, but they do make me curious. Think I'll build a torch and take a look at a few feet of one, jus' ta see where they go."

Quinn smacked his lips after slurping a taste from the pot. "You start, Phineas. I'll build another torch and follow you. Be careful, some of these mining shafts just drop off into a big hole. Make sure your feet know where's they is going. I want to finish my supper while it's hot. Gonna need it."

Quinn settled next to a log and his bedroll to finish the last of his stew. Fat was congealing along the sides of his cup, so he pushed it close to the fire to warm it up. Phineas disappeared into the shaft that radiated to their right from this central room.

"Funny, it's so neat in here. 'Spect they intended ta come back one of these days," Quinn said to no one in particular as he looked about the room, taking more time to inspect the place. He stirred his stew and watched Phineas' fading light disappear down the mineshaft.

He listened to the footsteps slowly echo away and the wavering glow of his torch fade to a dim light in the tunnel. Setting his empty cup down, Quinn tied some spruce knots together and lit them over the fire to follow. "Hope he's not lost. Hey, Phineas, I'm coming." He came to a low wall hanging down in the tunnel that he would have to bend over to get under. "Damn, my daddy tol' me to stay out of caves." Hearing a low whistle on the other side, he ducked under a rocky ledge to find Phineas staring before him, holding his torch high so he could see what lay before him.

"Whatcha find, Phineas?" Quinn was blinded by both torches blazing in the black hole of the cavern. He blinked and let his eyes adjust to the torch glow in the dead black of the room. What he saw left him speechless.

Phineas put his fingers to his lips and raised his torch and pointed to the walls of the room.

Hairs on Quinn's back and neck prickled. Sucking in a faint hiss, the blood left his face and washed down into his stomach, causing him to crouch down in wonder as he held his torch high and duckwalked in a circle as he took in the room, disbelieving the scene of what lay before him. An involuntary low whistle escaped Quinn's lips, but no words would form.

"What do it mean, Quinn? I ain't never saw anything like dis before," Phineas whispered as he stared around the room. His eyes grew round trying to see and make his mind assemble the images that lay before him. He put his hand on the short sword that hung at his side. "I been all aroun' da world an ain't never seen this afore."

"Me neither." Quinn stood fully erect and back-to-back, both men turned, looking at the enormous room they were in. "We ain't supposed to be here, Phineas. This ain't made for a white man's eyes to see."

"Aye. I don't doubt your word, but how do you know that?" Phineas' voice whispered in awe and a twinge of fear as it crept up his back.

"I seen markings like this down in Mexico. Aztec or Inca markings like I seen down there from some of the temples, but these is different. One of the officers had a book about Cortez and how he conquered the people who ruled Mexico at one time. There were pictures in the book that look like these marks.

Conquistadors came to California and did the same to the Indians, took their gold, and turned all the people into slaves. I read about it whilst I was in the Army. This place is sacred. Don't disturb anything."

Quinn held up his torch to look at something on a wall. "Well, I'll be." He held his flame up to find another torch protruding from the wall. It ignited readily. Then he found another sticking out from the wall and lit it. A low blue flame crept along the end of the torch gaining strength and illuminating more of the room. "Someone has been working in here."

Phineas followed Quinn's example and found several more torches mounted on the wall in similar fashion. They lit another and another until the room was bathed in a yellow flickering light, bright enough to see with.

"This is why I say, we shouldn't be here, Phineas." He pointed his toe at a body sitting on the floor clad in ancient Spanish armor. Two sticks were thrust through the man's eye sockets. A bit of hair clung to the white skull. His dusty, tattered clothing covered bare bones beneath the boots and armor.

Bodies covered in blankets were interred into the walls in open crypts. Pottery, tools, woven cloth, and weapons lay about the floor in orderly fashion. Painted figures in brown and black, accented with crimson red adorned the yellow ochre-colored mud stucco covering the walls of the room.

"Don't touch nothing. This must be the burying place for the ones that escaped, is what I'm guessing. I had read where a large group of Indians had gotten away. Families with children, carrying their goods and gold with them. They sent soldiers to find them. Must of found 'em. That could be one of them soldiers with the sticks in his eyes if I'm right."

"There's hundreds of crypts in des walls." Phineas tried to estimate how many, as he turned and cast his eyes on the unbelievable sight. "Hundreds."

"I bet we find more of the same in the other rooms. They must have established some kinda village close by and could a survived for generations in these mountains."

"Quinn?"

"What is it, Phineas?"

"Dis one is fresh. I mean newer dan de others. Look." Phineas was examining a body in a wall crypt about waist-high. The chambers were chiseled out of the rock wall three levels high. Each chamber was about six feet long, two feet high, and two feet deep. Yellow ochre paint on the surface with old Indian glyphs decorated each internment.

"You're right, Phineas. This body ain't wasted away yet. Looks to be here maybe a few weeks. He could almost sit up an' talk to us. Not good. We must leave here as soon as this storm lets out. Or else..."

"Or else? Dinae know what ya mean by that?"

"That's what I mean," He thumbed over in the direction of the dead Spanish soldier. "Someone must be attending to these caves. That's why they look so clean and neat. Let's put these torches out and get back in the other room."

As he exited the passageway, Phineas held up his torch studying another passage. He looked over to Quinn. "Ya know, Iddie, would it matter to anyone if'n we was to take a peek into this other tunnel? I'd like to know if they are all the same." Raising his flickering torch a bit higher, he entered the tunnel on their right.

Quinn started after him with a protest on his lips. "Phineas…" But, he was gone.

Orange highlights bounced off the walls, reflecting the bright torch light Phineas held in fascination at the sight before him. He called to Quinn, "Hey, yoo need ta see this," and was blinded by Quinn's torch as he entered the room.

Quinn stood dumbfounded.

Golden coins piled in huge ceramic bowls glinted from thousands of flashing facets, bouncing off of stacks of native gold bars in a room that looked to be twenty feet deep.

"Holy mother of God," spilled from Quinn's lips. Their faces paled at the sight before them. Without a word, the men backed away and quietly went back to their fire.

Pushing his coffee cup close to the fire, Quinn filled it and sipped pensively. Looking over at Phineas, he said, "Tol' ya. We leave as soon as the weather lets up."

Silently, Phineas passed him the bottle. He sat with his sword laying across his lap, stroking it absentmindedly with a sharpening stone.

Quinn kept his pistol close at hand and rifle leaning up against the log. The silence in the cave had become an eerie presence, magnifying the sounds from their fire. Neither had spoken since they returned from the crypts, musing their own reflective thoughts, glancing over to the tunnel entrances occasionally, reassuring themselves they were alone.

"I don know dat I can sleep tonight, Quinn. They must be Indian spirits all about the place, I'm a thinking. We done seen the bodies and we seen the gold. Sights that will never leave me mind. They musta been digging in these caves for hundreds of years now. I don't wanta look no more. I don't want no more whisky either. Plays with my head, and right now? Me mind is going round and round in circles, 'bout ta drive me bat-shit looney."

"No more whisky? You are bothered! Though I feel it too. Spirits all around this place." He sat the bottle down next to his bedroll. "Gives me the shivers, it does. Speakin' of which, we haven't seen or heard or smelt any bats. Ain't natural. Bats and caves go together. Never been in a cave this big with no bats. Seems peculiar. Maybe that means someone is coming here more often than we know.

"Old Indians I have talked to say the ancient ones had lived here long before the Indian races were created by the Great Spirit. Lots of stories of ancient ones from so long ago, living all over the west. Flying Eagle told me that his tribes had ruled these mountains for thousands of years before time could be counted. They had found evidence of an ancient race living here long before they arrived. The winds had blown the ancient one's old cities to dust. Makes ya wonder. It's on my mind, we need to leave as soon as possible. Sleep if you can. I'm tending the fire all night."

◆◦◈◦◆

"Quinn. Wake up." Phineas reached out with his boot and kicked Quinn's foot.

Quinn sharply inhaled, brought out of a deep sleep and startled awake, snorting through his nose. "What? Whatcha done that for? I was sound asleep, Phineas. Let me be." He rolled over on his side and covered his head with his hat.

"Quinn, we got company," he hissed under his breath. He kicked him again. "Wake oop!"

Quinn slowly uncovered his head, looking at Phineas. "What you mean we got company?"

Phineas' face was half shadowed by the firelight. His bright eyes highlighted by the flames, flashed underneath the brim of his hat. He nodded. "There. Him there. He's the company."

Quinn followed Phineas' gaze.

166

A lone figure squatted by the fire playing with the embers with a slender stick. His eyes were open, steel gray in color, studying the flames as if in deep contemplation. White-silver hair wrapped with leather thongs fell across his shoulders. He could have been anywhere from thirty to a hundred for all that Quinn could see. The eyes were older than his face. Buckskin shirt and jacket with buckskin breeches and boots were all that he wore. A necklace of turquoise and black glass hung from his neck and he wore a plain leather band around his head. Silver turquoise rings flashed in the firelight as he stirred the fire with his stick.

The man looked up. "Greetings, my friends. You seek shelter from the storm?"

"Yes, we did." Quinn sat upright, his attention on the newcomer. "We come here to get out of the weather. It was the only place we could find. We was lucky to find it."

"Lucky? I wonder?" He nodded and a hidden shadow moved from against the wall and entered the tunnel Quinn and Phineas had explored the night before. He nodded again and a shadow from another side of the cave went over to the horses and began exploring their packs and saddlebags.

"Now look here. We disturbed nothin'. We realized this was a special place and we was going to leave in the morning." Quinn sat up strongly but spoke his words with respect. It was obvious to him they were surrounded by many dark warriors hidden in the shadows.

The man waved for Quinn to be silent. He sat quietly stirring the fire, studying the men before him. When he spoke to the shadows that waited in the background of the cave, it was in an Indian dialect.

Quinn's ears perked up. A dark silhouette slipped from the tunnel, coming close to the fire and spoke in the same dialect to the silver-haired man. The one searching their packs spoke in the same dialect. He thought some of it seemed familiar.

"How did you find this place?" The old one stopped stirring the fire and spoke straight forward, never raising his voice.

"I spied a dark opening through the trees when the wind blew. We was looking high and low for a place to shelter to get out of da storm."

The man studied Phineas for a moment. "You are a Scot, are you not?"

"Aye."

"Many men come here to plunder the wealth of our country. We kill all thieves."

Another voice spoke out of the darkness. The silver-haired man nodded.

"My warriors tell me, you are not thieves. I must take you at your word. Hospitality to strangers is a law amongst my people. Forget you have found this place. Speak of it to no one. If you are found here again, you will sleep with the others in the tunnels, though your death will not be as peaceful as theirs. We are finished. Go now."

He stood up. The continence on his face told them he would not tolerate them any longer than it took for them to pack.

Quinn went to put out the fire. The old one raised his hand to stop him. "We will take care of that. The men you seek have doubled back on the trail. They are evil men. I hope you find them. Forget you were ever here."

Neither Quinn nor Phineas spoke for the first few miles on the trail. It was labor for the horses to break through the freshly fallen snow in the gathering dawn and to keep to the narrow slippery rock face. They cast glances up into the rocks and back along the trail to see if they were followed.

"Ya know, Phineas, I didn't see any trail from those Indians. Wonder how they found us. How did they get to the cave? I never had nobody sneak up on me like that fella did. Phineas, I fear we saw some spirits back there."

"Aye spirits of flesh and blood who would have poked

our eyes out and ripped our livers out of us, while we were still breathing.'" He turned in his saddle to look behind them. "Why did they let us go?"

"We didn't take nothing. We didn't disturb their ancient burial site, except, we was there and found it by accident. He believed us. We wouldn't be here if he didn't."

"I'll never forget what just happened."

"Remember it if you will, but never tell a single person what just happened here."

"Now why would I ever want to do something like that? It is a grand story."

"Yes, it is. I understood what he said to his warriors. It was in some type of ancient dialect, but I could make it out. He asked them to check to see if we had disturbed the gold or disturbed the bodies of his ancestors. They have much gold hidden back there. If you tell anyone, you are sending them to a certain death.

Our curse is, we know it's there as well, just out of our reach. It'll play on my mind forever, knowing there's gold back there, knowing I'll be killed for certain if I go looking for it."

My daddy used ta say, men is crazy when it comes to gold. I think I know what he was talkin' about."

Chapter 25

Two cold figures, mounted on their horses, huddled under a rocky outcropping, dark silhouettes against the bright whiteness around them. One had a collapsible looking glass, he was straining to see through the falling snow.

Lonnie turned to his dad. "I told you, Pa, they went up that mountain and disappeared into those trees. If we stay here, we freeze. I didn't want to go up into Yellowstone anyways. I like the desert. I say we double back and head for the old hideout. In a few hours, the snow will cover our tracks and they won't know where to find us. They'll be stuck up there and we'll be gone."

"It was my idea to hide out in Yellowstone. I looked forward to da hot bath and some buffalo hump roasting over da fire, but I think you is right, Lonnie. Dis is a good chance to get away. Dey won't know where to look after dis blizzard dat is a comin'. Le's go. If we get on de other side of the mountain, we be gone from here an we can find a place to camp 'til dis storm is over wit."

"Let's go, then. We still got a few supplies since we dumped that woman you wanted so bad. I was going to kill her after we got you out of the fort. Too bad she was crazy. I didn't trust she wouldn't cut our throats in our sleep, if we touched her. We can pass below where the posse is holed up and get away while it is snowing. Pa, we got to leave now."

"I know, Lonnie, but dat marshal is on ma mind. He kill John Paul. I bet he stay behind for dat girl too. You say there is only two of 'em up here in the mountain? I bet that boy is shacked up with that Voodoo woman. He may done got his throat cut too, I'm thinking. I wanna go see. He kill John Paul and he took off ma two fingers and stove up ma neck and ma head. I owe him big-time."

The sun was slipping behind the mountain when Lonnie and Angelle retraced their trail and passed below the fading tracks in the snow going up the mountain from Quinn and Phineas' climb.

"Keep da horses quiet as we go pass. Don' wanna give ourselves away."

Da'vid Angelle led the way with Lonnie bringing up the rear, leading the pack animal. They disappeared over the saddle in the pass as all light went out in the valley below.

Shepherd heard her moving under the bed covers. He continued drinking his coffee, nursing a feeling of dread over what he knew was coming, considering what the behavior of the woman had been before. She was quiet so far. He sipped the coffee, not turning to look at her. The tension in the room grew so thick he could have cut it.

"How did I get here and where is my damn clothes!"

Storm clouds were breached. Thunder and lightning flashed, shuddering the little cabin with screams of outrage and defilement.

"How dare you do this! God damn men to hell! Give me my clothes. I swear, boy, I'll cut your black dick off. Cotton picker! Give me my clothes. If I have to come out of this bed, I'll cut you so bad, your own mammy won't recognize you.

"Give me my clothes!"

"They're drying over by the fire." Shepherd kept his back to her, trying to give her some privacy, and he wasn't sure if she was covered at all. Her rage was something to hear.

"You undressed me?"

"I had no choice. You were freezing. I had to get you warm or you would have died."

"So you stripped me bare-ass naked and never touched me? You lying..." She wrapped the blankets around her and got up on the far side of the bed.

"Well, I did once." He shrugged.

"Damn men to hell. You're all alike. Take advantage of a helpless woman. Bastards."

"As I was saying... I touched you just once, to wipe a warm cloth across your face to clean off your witch mask."

"And I was naked and that's all you did?"

"The lady's attendant was out of the room." Shepherd chuckled behind his hand at his ironic statement. He looked at her stoically.

Hannah pursed her lips and exhaled through her nose, causing the tuft of hair dangling over her forehead to blow up and down. "Lady's attendant? Get out. Get out, so's I can dress."

"Yes, ma'am. Coffee is on the stove. By the way, check yourself over. No one in this room has touched you."

"Get out."

"I'll be on the porch."

"Get out now." A woman's boot swished close to Shepherd's left ear and banged against the wall. He ducked away and came back to a standing position with his hands up in the air. After bowing at the waist, he turned to her and tipped his hat.

She raised another shoe to throw. "Don't you look at

me."

"Hurry, will you, its cold outside." He closed the door firmly.

Shepherd pulled the makings for a smoke. Half ashamed for laughing at her consternation and the other half, proud at the way he had handled the entire episode. He settled himself on a log under the old porch and looked about at the beauty surrounding him, slowly rolling the tobacco and paper together. He grinned. "Hannah."

There is something about the mountains when they were dressed in white. A cleanness he had only experienced in the desert prevailed here, intriguing him. Perhaps it was the perceived perfection, a display of innocence that captured his attention. Perfection so rarely beheld. Beauty may be in the eye of the beholder, but Mother Nature didn't care what mortal man thought of her work. She freehanded her gifts and piled velvet snowflakes deep on green boughs, rocking them with gentle breezes, dusting chickadee and cardinal alike.

Rabbits burrowed in the feathery down, forming highways beneath the crusts, out of the eyesight of hawk and owl. Foxes hopscotched about, poking their noses into the fluff, sniffing for the scents of a supper of mice and voles. Bears slept in nests of leaves and duff unaware of the snow, lulled by the silence and deep cold into long slumber and solitude. The hand of nature ruffled the mountainside, sweeping her winds before her as she rolled and dusted with her snow clouds, oblivious of the creatures beneath. It was her time and she reveled in it.

Shepherd exhaled clouds of tobacco smoke into the cold air and drew in a deep breath of clean, spruce-scented air. He felt a strange quiet about himself. Somehow, he was at peace with the woman in the cabin. Why she intrigued him, he could not figure out. She had done nothing but abuse him and cause him trouble, even tried to cut him.

They were trapped here until the snow abated. He

hoped the cabin wouldn't be too small for the two of them, and some kind of peace could be reached. He did not want to chase her anymore. What sleep he had the night before had been interrupted each time he had got up to tend the fire. A good night's sleep would be welcome, if he could convince her not to cut his throat while he slept. He knocked on the doorframe, feeling the cold, hard, unyielding wood vibrate, hoping she was going to let him in.

No answer. He rapped a little stronger and opened the door. He was surprised it opened. He peeked in, ready to leap out of the way of any flashing knife.

"Come in. I won't hurt you." Hannah sat at the table drinking coffee. "I helped myself to your potatoes and beans you left from last night. I was hungry, still am."

Shepherd held his hand up. "Truce?"

"Truce." Hannah wiped her mouth with a bit of cloth then laid it on the table. "I'll clean these up."

Shepherd stood speechless as she bustled around tidying up. She took a pot, filled it with snow from out on the porch, then sat it on the stove to warm, so she could wash dishes.

"You might chop up some more wood on the porch, we're running low in here."

Shepherd stared at her, nodding.

"Well?" She looked at him, hands on her hips.

"Yes, ma'am, yes, ma'am." Grinning a little to himself, he split wood on the porch using his bowie knife and a small log for a baton, until he had enough and carried it in, stacking it close to the stove. The table was neat. The floor was swept. The bed was made. Her hair was pulled back out of her face.

"Don't get any ideas. I just like things picked up and neat."

"You okay? This ain't how you was before?"

"I tried to scare the hell out of you."

"Yes, and you did. Three or four times, at least, as I recall. One of them, by throwing yourself in a mountain stream."

"You don't sound like no field hand."

"I ain't no field hand. I was a house boy. Now I'm a man."

The peals of her mocking laughter sent chills up his back, reminding him of her mad laughter from the day before. Was it only one day? Had she gone mad again? He blinked at her, eyes wide not understanding her actions. "What are you laughing at?"

"Once a slave, always a slave. No matter where ya be."

"I used to think that way. Out here, it's different. Out here, I think of myself as a free man, before I think of myself as a black man and I don't think about it no more. I just do. I can hold my own with anyone."

Hannah looked at him, shaking her head. "You're still a man and in my book, that means you ain't worth the powder to blow you up."

"That may be. Sounds like you had it rough. Well, lady, we all have had it rough one way or another. But we is still alive and that counts for something to my way of thinking. You haven't lived my life and I haven't lived yours. You don't know what I've done or had done to me. Fight me and I'll fight you. Work with me and I'll give all I can to help. But cross me and we're on the outs. Do so at your own peril." He hung his coat on the chair next to him. "I risked my life for you at least twice now. Why, I don't know. That should mean something. It's going to take a while for us to trust each other. Out here, you can outlive your past and make a new tomorrow, if you're willing."

"Don't lie to me to impress me. I know men. They all liars and betrayers. You're no better. Just warning you now. Come within an arm's reach of me, and I'll cut you. I don't care if you're reaching for the salt. Get near me and I'll make you sorry. Your arm will come back a bloody nub.

I've warned you."

"I hear you. I buried the Thompsons by the way. That's how I got on your trail. I've been after Lonnie and Angelle for some time now."

Hannah paused wide-eyed, her face a blank. "You did that? The Thompsons were the nicest folks I ever knew. I'm thankful that you saw to them." She sat down, tilted her head, and looked up at him. "Who are you?"

"The name's Shepherd, United States Deputy Marshal." He tipped his hat. "At your service, ma'am."

"Deputy Marshal? You lying."

"No. Look here." He turned his vest lapel and displayed his marshal's badge.

She looked at it then his face. "It's real?"

"Yes, Hannah, it's real. I'm real too. I've told you no stories. No lies. I am who I say I am. No tricks to trace. All my cards are on the table."

"You want cards on the table? My specialty. I been a white man's whore since I can remember. The last bastard that owned me was a riverboat gambler on the Mississippi. He taught me to play poker and I was better than him and he finally backed me and let me play. I made him a lot of money.

"One night he got drunk and I bet him my freedom, playing high card wins. We had witnesses around the table. I won. I made him sign my papers right then and there.

"As we got close to St. Louie one night, drunk as the skunk he was, he tried to tear them up and make me his whore again and go back working the tables. Seems his winnings was cut down, because I was playing for myself by then. We fought. I cut his throat and pushed him over the side. They suspected me, but, they could never find no body. No one saw me and no one could prove nothin'."

Shepherd turned, giving her his full attention. "I'm listening." She continued with a look of doubt on her face; maybe this would get her into more trouble. "I told them he was probably drunk and fell overboard. A few believed me, but some didn't. By the time we got to St. Louie, the white captain decided I was the only one who would have done it and tried to get a constable after me. I hightailed it off that boat with a valise full of money and the clothes on my back.

"I met up with the Thompsons, who hid me out and took me with 'em. We done good, till Lonnie found us broke down with a busted wheel out on that gawd-awful desert. What he done to my friends, I never want to see again. I don't trust no man. That includes you, Shepherd Marshal. Stay clear of me."

"Aw, you remembered my name at least. It's a beginning. You can call me Shepherd. Last name is McKinzey, everybody called my daddy, Mack. Marshal is kinda formal, don't you think?"

"I don't care what your name is. How we gonna get outta this place?"

"Decided to live, huh. Good, that's good. Tired of chasing you around, myself. From the looks of the weather, this place is the best we can do for a day or so. If it gets worse and we get snowed in, not so good. Not enough food for more than a week of short rations, unless I get a deer or an elk. Maybe there's some sheep or goats up in these mountains too. Also, I'm worried about my friends out there in this weather. Should have made them stay, but you scared 'em off with your witch act."

"They men, ain't they? I don't give damn about your friends. What we got to eat? I'm still hungry. That Angelle wouldn't feed me unless I put out for him. I didn't get many meals. Lord, he's a big man."

"We can make biscuits. Did I ever tell you about my biscuits? I'm the best biscuit maker this side of the Missouri river. Got some peaches, beans, some canned meat, canned milk, bacon, always got bacon, pemmican, and desiccated dry vegetables. Oh, there's jerky and some dried plums. Help keep ya regular on the trail."

"Help keep me regular? Who do you think I am, your patient?"

"I've been known to doctor a few souls. Used to do it on the old estate, many lives ago." Shepherd turned away from her and stared at the flames in the stove. His mind raced through long forgotten memories. Absentmindedly, his fingers tapped his knees. Faces of friends he would never see again flashed in crystal-clear relief. Voices he hadn't heard in years sounded as fresh as the moment they were uttered.

"Whew, hey, hey, Shepherd." Hannah snapped her fingers in front of his face. "You just left me there. Come back."

"Huh? Oh, just some long forgotten thoughts is all. Your words seemed to bring them flooding back. Funny. Sorry. You ain't the only one with a past." Shepherd looked at her for a moment then around the room. "You cook?"

"Passable. I'll cook the supper. You make your biscuits. They had better be good or you can clean up."

"I'll bet you wash and I'll watch." He started to go past her then thought better of it and walked around the table, moving over to his stash of provisions.

"Bet what?"

"Whoever wins at cooking. My biscuits against...whatever you cook. Winner washes the dishes, girl. That's what I said. Not trying to trap you. To make it fair, we both get a vote." Shepherd laughed and went to making his biscuits.

Hannah dug around and came up with canned beans and canned meat. "You ever had New Orleans red beans, boy?" Hannah smiled a little.

"I done eat every kind of bean, but I never had a New Orleans beans to tell you the truth."

"Well, you will tonight. Make you slap your mama."

Shepherd paused what he was doing, looking up at her.

"I never saw my ma after I was ten. Wouldn't think of slapping her."

"Sorry, Shep. It's just an expression we use to say if something is very good. I lost my ma too. I was nine."

"Well let's cook for them, then." Shepherd smiled at her and went back to mixing his biscuits while he sat at the table.

* * *

Hannah stopped what she was doing, looking down on Shepherd's bowed head as he worked. *He's a fine-looking man,* she thought to herself. Biting her lip, she went on with her cooking.

After dinner, Shepherd pushed back his chair and patted his stomach.

Hannah appreciated the satisfied look on his face.

"Those were some fine beans, Hannah. Not too spicy either."

"I did like your biscuits as well, Mr. Marshal. I am sure full. Haven't had a full belly in a long time."

"How about I wash and you dry, then?" Shepherd put a pot of water on to boil.

As he walked behind Hannah, she moved her chair and looked at him sharply.

"Sorry, Hannah, no offense, just going to the stove. Didn't mean to get so close."

"I wasn't fooling around, Shepherd. I meant what I said."

"I know you did and I respect it. An arm's length? Been trying to keep it too."

"Where you sleeping tonight?"

"I figured I'd make a pallet on the floor under the table close to the fire."

"I sleep with my knife, you know."

"I assumed you would. I sleep with my gun. I warn

you, try to cut me again and I will defend myself. You've tried it twice, and I understand why, but I've done nothing to offend you. So behave. If I have to get up, it's to tend the fire or go outside for a call of nature, don't be alarmed."

"Me too, so don' get any ideas I'm coming to your bed if you hear me up."

"Never crossed my mind."

"Shepherd?"

"Yes, girl."

"Thanks for pulling me out of the creek. G'night."

"Hannah. I got something else for you." Shepherd moved over to his saddlebags.

"What could you have for me? We just met. Don't you go trying to trick me with no fancy presents. I don't fool easy."

"Here, Hannah. I found your doll and your journal. Your picture is there, too. An, I been keeping this in my pocket. It smells nice. Brings back a lot of memories." He placed the sachet on top of her journal, put them on the table, and stepped away.

Hannah sat on the bed staring at Shepherd, and then at the small pile of her beloved items she never thought she would see again. Slowly, she gathered them in her arms and lay down on the bed, her back to him.

"You're welcome. Pleasant dreams, Hannah. Pleasant dreams." He laid his pistol down by his bed.

CHAPTER 26

S hepherd woke early and put on his hat, shirt, and boots, stirred the fire to life before setting a pot of coffee on to boil, then sat and wiped down his rifle with a rag.

"Whatcha doing, Shepherd?" Hannah held her bedclothes up between her arms across her chest as she sat up in bed, her hair in disarray, wiping the sleep from her eyes.

"Thought I'd see if I could find some fresh meat. Give you a chance to dress while I'm gone and cook a little breakfast. Coffee will be ready in a little while. Save some for me, will you? I like it sweet and with some of that canned milk." He pulled on his coat, took his rifle in his right hand, and turned to her before he went out the door. "I expect a thick steak, fried potatoes with onions fried crisp and brown. Sourdough pancakes with hot maple syrup and butter just a oozing between the stacks and a half dozen fried eggs when I get back. Got it?" He winked a merry wink, closing the door in her exasperated face.

"Steak? Sourdough pancakes? Maple syrup? Who the hell do you think you are ordering me around, you jackass." She threw her pillow at the door. "Thinking I'm going to wait on him?" She paused and felt a wee smile twitch her lips. "He was joking. He was funnin' me! A man hasn't made a joke with me for, a... I can't remember when."

She lay back down and silently laughed to herself, until she realized she had a big smile on her face. She wasn't sure if she was smiling at his joke or at the many times she missed out on having someone to make her smile. "I think I've been a fool." She turned on her side and stared at the wall, brushing the tears away in embarrassment. "I better get dressed."

Hannah bustled around the cabin, putting things in order. After wiping off the table, she spread one of her dresses like a tablecloth for them to eat off of. Blowing with pursed lips, up through her hair as she sat, she helped herself to a cup of strong coffee fixed just the way Shepherd had told her he enjoyed his. "Sourdough cakes and maple syrup sure sounds fine. I hope he finds something. Fresh meat would taste mighty good, even if we ain't got no maple syrup." She sipped her coffee and wondered what it might be like to be Shepherd's woman.

Feet stomped the snow off of boots outside the door and the handle jiggled up and down. Pulling back her hair then tucked in her blouse, she laughed as she flung the door open. "Welcome back," she called. A black shadow filled the doorway.

"Glad I is to see you too, gal. I see your man is gone from dis place. He must be hunting. He owes me a life, now I is gonna take you with me and when he come for you, I gonna make him pay for my John Paul."

Hannah's scream started in the pit of her stomach and burst from her mouth, only stopping when Angelle slapped her face and she collapsed in a fainted heap on the freshly swept, cold cabin floor.

◆◦◈◦◆

Shepherd carried the small mule buck across his shoulders, careful with his steps so he wouldn't fall. The buck wasn't very big, maybe a hundred fifty pounds or so, but a great find for him and Hannah. If he dropped it, it would be difficult to get the dead weight back across his shoulders and would have to be dragged. Shepherd had gutted the deer to be rid of extra weight, but had saved the liver, kidneys, and heart. This would make a tasty stew and bring some relief to the diet they had been sharing of dried and canned food.

He was elated, enjoying a sense of bringing food home to a family. His family. Somehow, it made him feel stronger, this feeling in his chest. He was the provider, the one she depended on.

He was probably a damn fool for thinking this way, but another part of his becoming a completed man slid into place in the puzzle of his life. *Damn, is this what love is like?*

Breaths came in short gasps as he climbed the slippery stairs to the cabin and pushed against the door. He laid the carcass down on the floor and looked up, brushing his hands off before setting his rifle on the table.

"See what I brung ya?"

Silence.

He looked around, rubbing his eyes as if they were deceiving him. She couldn't have run off again. His heart had told him she was coming over to his side. She was nowhere to be seen. Her clothes were gone and the rag of a coat she had worn was gone. "She did run off. The damn little fool. That's it. I'll have nothing to do with a crazy woman."

He opened the door to the cabin and looked around. Tracks in the snow led down the mountainside and to the trail toward the Green River.

"Hannah! Hannah!" he called. His voice boomed against the steep sides of the mountains, echoing his plaintive cry. Crossing around behind the cabin, he went to check to see if she had taken a horse. They all were there.

"She didn't take a horse?" Burro nudged him for a rub. Absentmindedly, he played with the little animal's ears. Shepherd stood perplexed. "What has happened here?" He was confused. "She didn't leave on her own. Someone must have taken her, then."

Running to the tracks going down the mountain, he knelt to examine them. One large horse and two smaller ones! *Angelle!* He stood up looking down the mountain for any movement, but there was only snow and trees and mountains, coldly mocking him. He had never felt so alone, even when he was locked up in the smokehouse, back on the plantation. A horse blew through his nose behind him. He swiftly turned toward the sound, pulling the hammer back on his rifle, his eyes alert.

"Thought we'd find you shot to rags." Quinn sat his horse a few steps behind him.

Phineas pulled up next to Quinn. "It's Angelle and Lonnie, Shepherd. They doubled back on us."

Shepherd lowered his gun with a sigh of relief.

"We've been followin' them for several days. Kinda puzzled us when they turned off the main trail and headed back here. Glad to see you're in one piece." Phineas spat into the snow.

"He came back for her, didn't he? He came back for the witch. He must be crazy. At least you're rid of her." Quinn sat his horse, waiting for Shepherd's response.

"I don't want to be rid of her. I love her. I think she loves me. Glad to see you, boys. Gotta go. Come or follow, it makes no never mind to me. I'm going to kill Angelle. If he has hurt her, I'll burn him alive over a hot fire. Maybe a little at a time, just to see the juices run out of him as he screams."

CHAPTER 27

━ ◆ ◈ ◆ ━

S hepherd threw his gear together while Quinn and Phineas finished butchering the buck and wrapped the boned meat in the hide.

"Not going to let fresh meat go ta waste. Shepherd, ya know you can't go out there without us." Quinn secured the filled hide behind his saddle.

"Aye, Quinn. I dinnae think we should let him go out there in the heat he is in. He's liable to melt the mountainside and start an avalanche." Phineas threw a wink Quinn's way.

"I suspect you is right. We gotta go. What kinda spell did she use, Shepherd, to get you so worked up?" Quinn crossed his arms over his saddle horn, spit in the snow, and studied Shepherd's face.

"She's no crazy woman. She just tried to scare us. I've been in love with her since I read her journal and saw her picture back on the desert. Being alone with her in this cabin, only let me know I was right. I don't know why, but I think she's trying to fall in love with me. Ready? I'm leaving. All they've got is a few hours head start."

"Lead da way, me bucko. I want to end this chase as much as you, but for different reasons. I want a warm bed an' a roof over me head and sleep for a month when this is over."

"That's true, Phineas. They've led us a merry chase. I'm tired of chasing. Never had it so hard to catch some fellas. Sides, I want ta get away from here." Quinn looked back over the ridges toward the mountain cave. "I got an itch I won't be able ta scratch if I stay here. We're following you, Marshal. Just don't get too wild-eyed. Angelle came back here and got that gal to bait you. He plans on killin' you. Don't forget that."

Snow was knee-deep to the horses back on the main trail. They snaked out single file behind Angelle's broken tracks through the deep stuff. For two days, they followed those tracks down the mountain. Once they left the heights, they could see more clearly. The snow was only scattered across the plains in deep tufts. The wind swept most of the flatland clear.

Shepherd urged Dusty forward. As they dropped down into the valley of the Green, Shepherd waved a halt, surveying the broad, boulder-strewn plain in front of them.

"What do you make of that, Quinn?" About a quarter of a mile in front of them, a fire blazed on the riverbank. No one was in sight.

"Don't know. Don't see nobody. Looks like they saw us coming and skedaddled. They run off in a hurry seems like. Left a bunch of rags and such tied to a pole by the fire. Seems peculiar ta me, them leaving some sort a signal like that."

Shepherd stood up in his stirrups. "Them ain't rags, that's Hannah." Spurring Dusty ahead, he shot off with the others close behind. He had to go around the large boulders in the field, but he only had his eyes on Hannah! She was screaming at him, but his blood was up and he couldn't make out what she said.

"No, Shepherd, don't come!" Her voice finally broke through to him. "He's waiting for you behind the boulders.

Don't come. Go back." Her voice bounced off the rocks and got caught up in the wind, before reaching Shepherd's ears. Her cries were mixed anguish and tears, which only spurred him on.

His eyes never left her figure. He knew death was lurking behind a large boulder somewhere close to her. An enraged beast, waiting for prey.

Lonnie lay flattened out on a rock shelf about ten feet in the air, waiting for the men to come into range. The hunted had turned to hunting and the prey was Shepherd, Phineas, and Quinn charging into their trap.

A coldness settled on her heart as she watched them ride into the trap. She watched transfixed by the drama playing out in front of her.

Angelle had a large club about four foot long in his hand. He told her he was going to knock Shepherd off of his horse, then stomp and beat him to a bloody pulp. He laughed as he set himself in position.

Lonnie lined up his first shot.

She gasped when Phineas nearly lost his saddle as the bullet nicked his right shoulder. He screamed, but he held on. She held her breath as Quinn and Shepherd swerved their horses at the sound of the shot. Quinn broke left and Shepherd right.

To her right, Shepherd's sudden move caught Angelle off guard. He was on the wrong side of the boulder!

Screaming obscenities in Cajun French, Angelle reversed his swing, only to swing high, brushing Shepherd enough to knock him off of his horse.

Phineas headed for Hannah, dismounted quickly, and stumbled a few steps as he made his way to her to cut her free.

"Run, Shepherd, run. He going to kill you. He's mad,

mad, mad!" Her voice broke in the clean mountain air until it was rendered to a squeaky lisp. She kept trying to warn him, after her voice left her. "Run, run. Why won't you run?" she wisped.

Phineas cut her bonds then grabbed her around the waist as she attempted to run to Shepherd.

"No, no, Lassie. I got you. Easy, I say. You cain't help 'em. Believe me when I tell you. Dat Angelle has bit himself off a man ta chew on."

They both collapsed onto the ground. Hannah cried in anguish. Phineas's left arm held her fast as they watched the fight.

Quinn circled around to help Shepherd, riding up behind him.

"Quinn," Shepherd shouted. "Take Hannah home for me if I don't come out of this. Promise?"

"I promise, Shep, but I'll kill this bastard if you don't make it."

"You won't need to. I'm going to do it right here and now." A rifle shot kicked up rocks and dust at Quinn's feet.

Quinn fought to control his horse, "Whoa Bob! Excuse me, I forgot about the rat shit spawn still in the wood pile. Say good-bye to Lonnie, Angelle. That little man is mine." He galloped for the prostate Lonnie on his ledge, handgun drawn and firing.

"He kill you, Mister. I know ma Lonnie." Da'vid called after Quinn.

Quinn rode off, zigzagging the boulders, racing for Lonnie's position.

"Shepherd!" Hannah's voice rallied and fell upon the wind.

"I knowed dat gal bring you to me. Now I kill you, jes as I promised my John Paul." Angelle swung his club like an axe.

Shepherd ducked the blow, and pulled his bowie knife as he dove toward Angelle's feet, rolling on the ground, slashing at the giant's legs. He drew the first blood and Angelle hopped away on one foot.

"A little sting like that don't hurt me." Angelle limped toward Shepherd again, club raised to break and crush his victim into pulp. "Kee Yiiii."

The club arced in the air and fell, catching Shepherd on the wrist, knocking the knife from his hand and spun him around toward where Phineas had Hannah wrapped in his arms. He tripped and fell at Hannah's feet.

"Oh, Shepherd. Run, Shepherd. Please run!" she cried hoarsely and kicked, trying to pull herself from Phineas' grasp.

"Hey, girl. Thought you'd left me again. I'll be right back." He grinned to her then rolled over on his back, avoiding the next blow as it thudded in the frozen ground, and kicked Angelle in the groin with both feet.

Angelle gasped and stumbled back but didn't fall. He leaned on his club, bent at the waist fighting to catch his wind. "I got cojones of stone, boy. No man has ever stopped me."

Shots in the distance cracked in the air.

"Lonnie got your partner. Count on dat. Come on now, we finish dis." He raised the club over his head but changed his mind. "I'm going to crush you with my bared hands." He lunged at Shepherd, holding both fists closed, striking down at his shoulders, knocking him to his knees.

Shepherd rolled away to avoid being hit again then up on his feet out of reach of Angelle's massive arms. He stepped in and smashed a right to Angelle's jaw, causing the giant to shake his head in wonder. Then, a stiff left to his nose, which broke flat and laid it over on Angelle's face.

Shepherd danced back out of reach, as Angelle swiped at him with his right arm as he tried to clear his vision. He stepped in with a roundhouse right that shook Angelle to his core, but the big man didn't go down.

"Yo strong." Angelle gasped. "But I is stronger." He blew the blood out of his nose. The cartilage cracked as he straightened it and he blew the blood out again. "Now I ken breathe. I like pain. It make me mad."

Doubling his ham-sized fists, he moved toward Shepherd, swinging blows left and right, advancing with unrelenting force and power. Shepherd moved and slipped, taking hard hits to his ribs and shoulders.

"He's going to kill him," Hannah pleaded with Phineas. She looked him in the face, begging for his help, then saw the shoulder wound. "You're bleeding."

"Aye, Lassie, I got shot coming for yew. Ay'm bleedin' an feelin' weak a bit from that liddle scratch." He took a short painful breath and whispered, "If Shepherd loses, an I am out of the fight. Take this." He pulled his short sword out of his belt. "It's slick and sharp as my second wife's tongue. Wait 'til the beastie gets close, den stooff it in his guts." His eyes rolled back in his head and Phineas passed out.

Hannah laid him down gently on the ground and picked up the sword from his hand. She held it to her side in a white-knuckled death grip, and watched the fight in a trance.

Shepherd was on one knee in front of the behemoth. Angelle towered over him, raining blow after blow to Shepherd's back. As Angelle bent to hit him again, Shepherd exploded from his kneeling position using his legs like a piston. He landed a ground-to-sky uppercut that broke a young boy's neck many years ago. It caught Angelle in the throat and soft flesh between his jaws, and crushed the big man's larynx.

Shepherd followed with a flurry of body punches to the huge belly. Angelle gasped, but couldn't suck in any air. His face turned purple. Flailing in the air, he turned and fell onto Hannah, and grabbed for her throat.

She screamed as they rolled over and over on the

ground. An elbow to his face broke his grip and, she pushed away from him, tearing his hands from around her neck. She revealed her sword and waved it in his direction, hissing in her vilest voodoo accent, "Hecate's curse upon you as I send you to hell."

Disbelief shown in his eyes and an agonized "Oomph" escaped from his mouth when she sliced the belly of the big man to his backbone with the razor-sharp sword. "Where you get dat," he gasped.

Angelle fell away from her, his eyes bulged as he fought to hold his guts together. He sucked bubbling, bloody froth down his throat and died, strangled on his own swallowed tongue.

"Like soft butter," she said, kicking herself away from the monster with her feet. She ran to Shepherd.

Shepherd stumbled toward her, as he saw her kick Angelle over with his guts spewing out over the snow and rock. He fell on one knee in front of her and she ran into his arms, sobbing. She kissed his face and shoulders. He caught her by the back of her neck and crushed her to him in a lingering deep kiss that left no doubt about his feelings.

"I suppose this means, you're in love with the crazy lady." Quinn's voice broke their moment.

"Yeah, Quinn, I'm in love with the crazy lady." Shepherd grinned and tightened his grip on her. "You're never going to get away from me again." He hugged her and kissed her again.

She nestled into his embrace. "I don't want to never leave."

"Where's Phin? I don't see him." Quinn stood up in his stirrups.

"Oh! Sorry, Shepherd, I gotta see to another man." She got up off of his knee. "He's over there. He passed out after cutting me free. He's been shot. Help me with him, will you?" She ran over to Phineas' still form and began pulling his clothes away from his wound.

"His shoulder is still seeping blood. The bullet passed through. We'll have to cauterize it." Shepherd felt for a pulse. "He is still alive. I'll use my knife."

After wiping the blade with snow to clean it, he laid it on the fire until it glowed bright cherry red then placed it deliberately on Phineas' right shoulder.

Phineas came to from the pain with a start, looked at Shepherd, a mask of hate on his face. "Ah, man! You be burnin' me! May the fairies twist your nose and cause your land to be barren, ye back stabbin' British scum!" Recognition passed through his eyes and he looked from face to face. "We musta won." His eyes rolled back into his head and he fell across Hannah's shoulder. She laid him down and covered him up, leaving the fresh wound exposed, afraid any cloth would stick on the freshly burnt skin.

"I trust you took care of Lonnie?" Shepherd looked up from Phineas to Quinn.

Quinn pointed to the shelf Lonnie had been shooting from. "I rolled a rock over on him where he fell. Better than he deserves. I'll drag Angelle over there and throw some rocks over him too. Most decent thing we can do, save the wolves from eating tainted meat."

"Going to be dark soon. Hannah, you mind camping here for the night? We'll leave first light."

"I will be wherever you are, Shepherd. Here will be fine. The night will cover the meanness that was, and the stars will shine down on us tonight."

CHAPTER 28

He held her in his gaze. "You goin' be alright. You've had it harder than the rest of us."

"I knew I was gonna be alright when I saw you comin' for me over that ridge. Most beautifullest sight I ever saw. Now can we eat? I'm starving."

"Will do, Hannah, brung you these. I thought you'd be wanting them." He removed her possessions from his saddlebags and handed them to her.

She took them and hugged them to her breast. "Shepherd. You are a surprise. Thank you."

"I brought home some fresh meat the other day, except you were gone, so we brought it with us. Quinn, put on some coffee and let's roast some meat for Hannah. Sit right there, girl." He pushed her down on a log in front of the fire. Pensively, he threw more wood on the fire, then grinned and said, "I will make you some biscuits. Did I ever tell you about my biscuits? I makes the best biscuits, this side of the Missouri river."

"Shut up, biscuit man." Hannah laughed, throwing her hands up. "You make my sides hurt. Quinn, you ever hear the like?"

"I been listening to his biscuit blather ever since he snuck onto my wagon train. Shoulda thrown him in the river. Now if you is to want a good cup of coffee, you just wait. I'm the best coffee maker around these parts."

"Stop, you two. Stop. I'm going to take this pot of hot water and go over behind that boulder. You both stay right here. I smell like a horse and am as hungry as one. Food had better be ready when I get back." She grabbed the bucket and walked away. "Don't go peekin'. You've both seen me mad."

"Yes, ma'am." They both turned to their work.

Shepherd cut spruce and pine boughs to make a deep bed and lean-to, then threw his bedroll on top of the gathered spruce boughs. "I guess that'll do for the night. Now for my biscuits." He began to dig through his saddlebags.

"She don't seem to be as crazy as I thought, Shepherd. You may have something there." Quinn glanced in her direction for a moment, and went back to making his coffee.

"I hope to find out, Quinn. I hope to find out." He started making his biscuits, looking over in Hannah's direction every now and then to make sure she was safe. Everything was cooking by the time Hannah returned.

Phineas came to with a start. After a moment, he realized where he was. He stared at his bloody sword lying next to him. "I see ya done me blade proud, Lassie. Proud of you, I am, even if you be a witch."

"I'll just let you keep thinking that way too," she told him. She checked his shoulder, placed a cloth over the proud flesh, and wrapped a sling around his shoulder.

"Is that necessary, Missy? This sling cramps me arm and I can't use it."

"That's the idea, Phineas. Don't use it. Your wound will open and you'll bleed. I'll have Shepherd burn it again if you like."

"No! I mean your meaning. Watch this one, Marshal. She is sly."

Quietly they ate their meal, Shepherd sitting as close to Hannah as he could without interrupting her eating. Phineas and Quinn exchanged knowing glances toward each other as they observed their companions.

"Phineas and I will just take our blankets and move way over there behind that ridge of rocks. Let you have the fire. I suppose you have a lot of talking ta do an it would jus keep us both awake." Quinn gathered up his saddle and blankets, gestured with his head for Phineas to follow.

"Aye, I'm plumb tuckered out, me self. Good night." One-armed Phineas picked up his saddle and blankets, lugging them against his leg.

"Be careful not to open that wound, Phineas. It'll start bleeding again," Hannah called.

"I'll see to it, Lassie." Both men faded into the night carrying their blankets.

"I'll carry those fer ya, Phinn."

"Naw, I's all right. Dinnae call me Phinn, I tol' ya."

Firelight flickered over their faces as they sat and watched the flames. They were quiet and sat apart from each other. Hannah drank some coffee and warmed her hands as she held the cup.

Shepherd rubbed his palms together, a thoughtful look on his face. He stifled a yawn every now and again. He looked up at the sky. "Stars are out. So big, you can almost touch them. I can't count them all. Look, Hannah, a shooting star. There, another. You see 'em?"

She followed his gaze. "Yes, I see them, Shepherd. The sky was never this big back east. Makes ya feel small, don't it?

"Like ya was part of something big. Don't it?" He looked at her.

She met his gaze then back to the sky. "They're pretty. Feels good by the fire." She held her hands out to warm them. "Makes me sleepy. Is that your bedroll over there?"

"Yeah, I made it up for you, thought I'd sleep next to

the fire close to you, if that's all right." He looked at the flames, rubbing the tops of his thighs with his hands. He cleared his voice and spoke again. "I'd like you to come home with me, Hannah. It's a long way to Oregon, but I think you'll like it there. I have this pretty cabin in the woods. I own half of a ranch and part of a grist mill, plus this job as marshal. I can afford to take care of you."

"You have a home?" She was looking at his face, searching his eyes.

"Yes, Hannah, I do. I'd like to share it with you."

"I've never had a home. No field hand could ever say that."

"I ain't no field hand." He spoke softly, wistfully, emptying his heart out to her, with a long look.

"I know. You're a marshal. A home? I always dreamed of havin' a home." She crossed her feet over each other and briefly stretched her arms over her head.

"I'd like to share it with you."

"Share your home with a voo doo woman. You crazy?"

He flushed and hung his head a little. "I don't know much about the voo doo stuff, but I'm crazy in love with you, Hannah. Yes, I'm crazy."

She cocked her head to the side and rested it on her fist, looking at him. "I believe you. I never been in love afore. I always hated the men who took me. Never got no chance to learn to love nuthin. Is love that feelin' what I felt, when I saw you riding to come get me?"

"I hope so."

"It made my stomach flutter. I felt safe and afraid, and, deep down, proud at the same time. Is that what it feels like?"

"Do your palms get sweaty and you feel a glow buildin' up inside you like you're gonna bust?"

"Yeah, I have that. I'm just not sure." She took his hand between hers, saw honesty in his eyes. "You know what I am?"

"I know what you was. If you come with me, we have all the time left in the world to find out what we will be."

She sat looking at him for a long time. "Suits me just fine." She looked at him again, shaking her head in disbelief, smiling up at the starry sky. "I like thinkin' on it. A home. Someone comin' home for supper, to me at the end of the day."

Hannah looked up into the sky again for a few minutes. She placed her hands on her knees, cocked her head to one side as she often did, and smiled at him. "I have an idea."

"What's that? Look another." He pointed to a streak glowing across the sky.

"They're beautiful, aren't they, Shepherd?"

"Yes, they are. Kinda like you." He stopped with words caught in his throat. "What's your idea?"

"My idea is for you to take that pail of warm water right there on the fire. Go find a nice boulder to bathe behind and come back and keep me warm tonight. You up for it?"

"I...er'...ah. You sure? I don't want to rush anything." He paused again. "You, you sure, Hannah?"

"That nervous tingle in my stomach feels kinda good. I like it. You'll find me in your bedroll when you come back. Wash good, I don't want you smelling like no field hand. I'm wondering what a real marshal smells like."

Shepherd watched firelight sparkle across her face and flitter in her eyes, as he weighed the words. "I...I...guess I better go, then. Can't keep a wondering mind a waiting." He stood, rubbed his hands together before picking up the bucket. He stopped and met her gaze. She looked back. "Guess, I'll go wash up." He disappeared into the still of the night, water sloshing his pant leg.

Hannah watched him go into the darkness. She looked

to the sky and stood then stretched her arms with hands fully clenched, turning around in a circle, filled to bursting with an inner feeling of delight and wonder. "I often dreamed it would be like this." Abruptly, she squatted with her hands over her head and sobbed her heart out.

After a short time, she wiped her face. Carefully, she took off her clothes folding them neatly. Kneeling before the fire, she waved smoke over herself to purify her body. Murmuring a short prayer to the stars overhead, she took a burning stick and etched a pentagram in the air before her. She completed her ritual by crossing herself over her chest then bowed her head and whispered a prayer. She stood, wrapped her arms around herself with the cold, then walked over to the bed of spruce boughs and crawled into Shepherd's bedroll. "This is nice and cozy. It smells of man. A good man. I like it." She propped herself up on her elbows watching for Shepherd to return.

Shepherd emerged from the dark into the firelight, his shirt wrapped around his waist. "Um, you ready, Hannah? I sure hope so, 'cause it's cold out here." He pulled back the blanket and lay down next to her. His shirt fell on the ground. Their bodies melded together like a fitted puzzle.

"Bein' honest with you, girl. I ain't done this in a long time. It's going to take some time to get the feel of it again. You smell good, spruce and smoke." He placed his left arm under her neck and his right arm over her waist, his hand on her back, looking into her face.

Hannah's voice was husky and quiet at the same time. Her eyes were lit by the firelight as she looked into Shepherd's face. "I can teach you, if you've forgotten anything, Shepherd."

"Oh, I remember everything, Hannah. I just meant, I'm going to take a long time warming up." He kissed her on the forehead.

She pressed into him, kissing him full on the mouth. "Take all the time you want." She moved her chest so her taut nipples brushed against his and pulled his right hand down between her legs. "Shepherd, I have never wanted a man to fill me up like I have been wanting you. That love feeling is washing all over me."

He kissed her, rolling her on her back. Taking her hard nipple between his lips, he bit softly, then harder, then soft, then hard again, causing a low gasp from her lips as the tightness grew into mounting pleasure. She looked at him, stroking his face with one hand, gripping his hard part with the other, aware that his right hand was exploring the soft places between her legs. The heat where he touched was mounting to a sizzling ache. Her breath was coming in intense spasms of air as she struggled to keep pace with his demanding hand.

"Who are you, Shepherd?" She moaned in a tiny voice, arching her back to allow the tantalizing fingers more room.

"I'm the man who loves you. I'm going to take my time, showing you that very thing." He kissed her breasts then lowered his head to kiss her stomach.

"Is this what love feels like, Shepherd?" she asked.

"Sometimes," he muttered between kisses to her soft stomach. "Sometimes it feels like this." He moved lower, intensifying his kisses as she raised her hips to meet his torturing lips.

Moaning in deep gasps, she pulled him on top of her. Passion hot and satisfying mounted into intense pleasure, as they moved as one, breathed as one, and shattered the night sky in a crescendo of blazing stars streaking across the universe before he collapsed on top of her, spent and numb from the loving.

They enjoyed their afterglow and the weight of them pressing together for a few minutes, then she squirmed away from him, turned her back to him, and then snuggled back against him in exquisite pleasure at the sparking touch of her skin against his. Her spirit at peace. She took his arm and wrapped it around her.

"You think I'm going to like Oregon, Shepherd?" she murmured to the sky as another star streaked across the heavens.

"Yes, I do, Hannah." he whispered in her ear, feeling the tiny hairs on the nape of her neck with his lips, tasting their wetness, their musk, tickle his lips. Pressing closer to her, he kissed her neck.

"I think so too." She wrapped his arms about her, pressing as close to him as she could. "Not bad for a U.S. Marshal."

ABOUT THE AUTHOR